Best in Children's Books

Garden City, New York 30

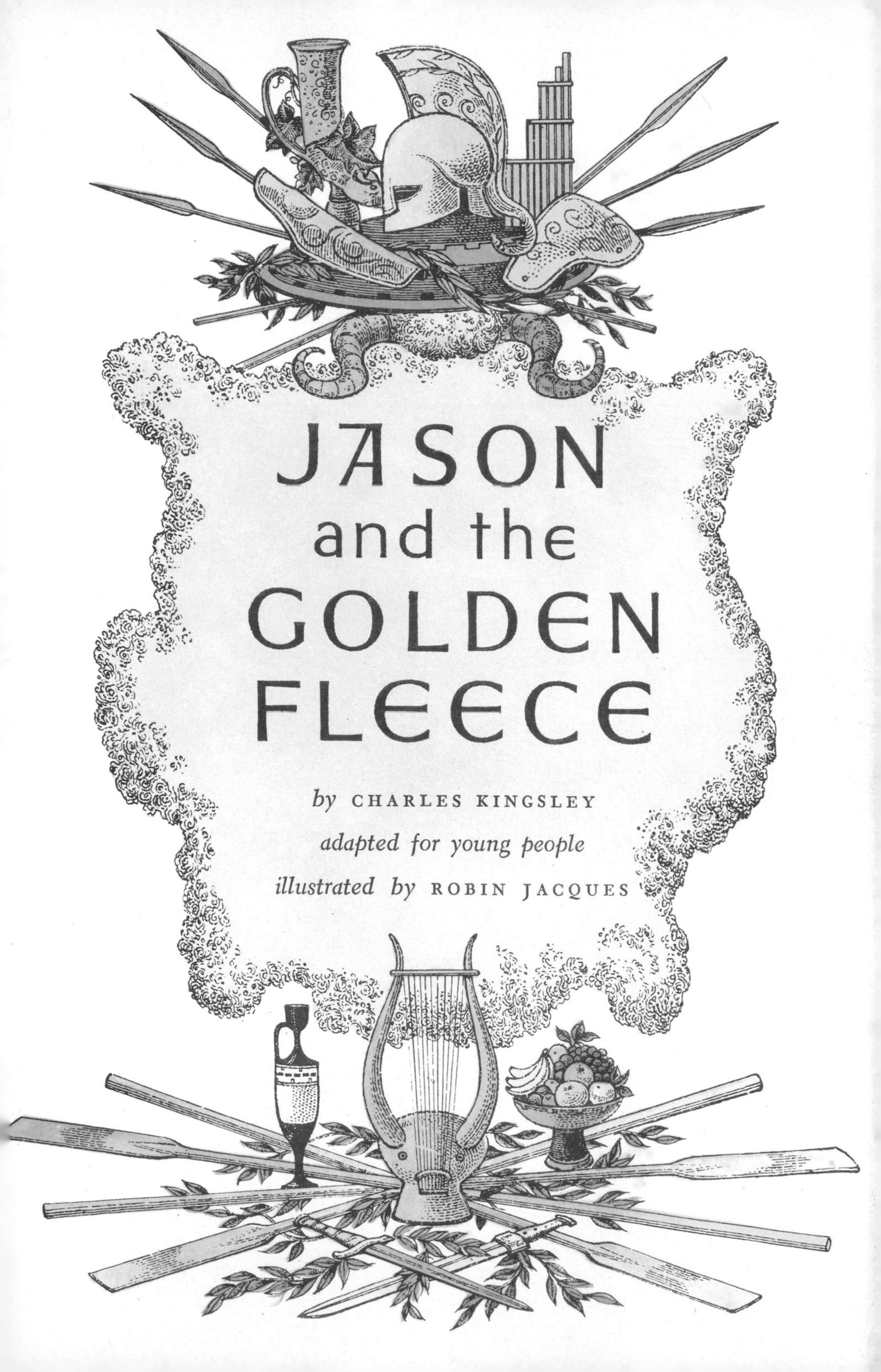

JASON and the GOLDEN FLEECE

by CHARLES KINGSLEY

adapted for young people

illustrated by ROBIN JACQUES

HOW JASON WAS TRAINED BY THE CENTAUR

I have a tale to tell you of heroes who sailed away into a distant land, to win themselves renown forever, in the adventure of the Golden Fleece.

And what was that Golden Fleece? The old Greeks said that it hung in Colchis, nailed to a beech tree in the war god's wood; and that it was the fleece of a wondrous ram that had come down from Mount Olympus, the home of the gods.

Now in another kingdom, far from Colchis, there dwelt a man called Aeson, who was king in Iolcos by the sea. But Aeson had a fierce and lawless brother named Pelias; and at last Pelias drove out Aeson, and took the kingdom to himself and ruled over Iolcos.

And Aeson, when he was driven out, went sadly away out of the town, leading his little son by the hand; and he said to himself, "I must hide the child, or Pelias will surely kill him because he is the heir."

So he went up from the sea, across the valley, through the vineyards and the olive groves, toward Pelion the ancient mountain. He went up and up the mountain, till he came at last to the mouth of a lonely cave.

Then Aeson said to the lad: "Here dwells the great and wise teacher, Cheiron the Centaur. With him you will be safe."

He led the boy into the cave where, upon bear skins and fragrant boughs, lay Cheiron, the ancient centaur, the wisest of all things beneath the sky. Down to the waist he was a man; but below he was a noble horse. His white hair rolled down over his broad shoulders, and his white beard over his broad brown chest.

He welcomed Aeson and the lad, saying: "I know you and all that has befallen you."

And Aeson said: "I entreat you in the name of Zeus, the father of gods and men, let the boy be your guest till better times, and train him among the other young men who are your pupils, that he may grow to heroic manhood and regain his father's kingdom."

Then Aeson wept over his son and went away.

So the lad became a schoolfellow to the sons of heroes: Achilles and Heracles and Orpheus and many another mighty name. He grew strong and brave and cunning, upon the pleasant meadows of Pelion, in the keen hungry mountain air. And he learned to wrestle, and to box, and to hunt, and to play upon the harp. And next he learned to ride, for old Cheiron used to mount him upon his back. And he learned the virtues of all herbs, and how to cure all wounds; and Cheiron called him Jason the healer, and that is his name to this day.

HOW JASON LOST HIS SANDAL

And ten years came and went, and Jason was grown to be a mighty man. And it happened, on a day, that Jason stood on a mountain; and Cheiron stood by his side.

And Jason looked south, and saw a pleasant land, with white-walled towns and farms, nestling along the shore of a land-locked bay; and he knew it for Iolcos by the sea.

Then he sighed, and asked: "Is it true what the heroes tell me, that I am heir of that fair land?"

"And what good would it be to you, Jason, if you were heir of that fair land?"

"I would take it and keep it."

"A strong man has taken it and kept it long. Are you stronger than Pelias the terrible?"

"I can try my strength with his," said Jason.

But Cheiron sighed, and said: "You have many a danger to go through before you rule in Iolcos by the sea, and many a woe, and strange troubles in strange lands, such as man never saw before."

"The happier I," said Jason, "to see what man never saw before."

And Cheiron sighed again, and said: "The eaglet must leave the nest when it is fledged. Will you go to Iolcos by the sea? Then promise me two things before you go."

Jason promised, and Cheiron answered: "Speak harshly to no soul whom you may meet, and stand by the word which you shall speak."

So Jason promised, and leapt down the mountain, to take his fortune like a man.

He went down through the arbutus thickets, till he came to the olive trees in the glen; and among the olives roared the torrent Anauros, all foaming with a summer flood.

And on the bank of Anauros sat a woman, wrinkled, grey, and old; and when she saw Jason, she spoke whining: "Who will carry me across the flood?"

Jason was bold and hasty, and was just going to leap into the flood; and yet he thought twice before he leapt, so loud roared the torrent, all brown from the mountain rain.

But the old woman whined again: "I am weak and old, fair youth. For Hera's sake, carry me over the torrent."

And Jason was going to answer her scornfully, when Cheiron's words came to his mind. So he said: "For Hera's sake, the queen of the gods on Olympus, I will carry you over the torrent, unless we both are drowned midway."

Then the old dame leapt upon his back, as nimbly as a goat; and Jason staggered in, wondering; and the first step was up to his knees.

The first step was up to his knees, and the second step was up to his waist; and the stones rolled about his feet, and his feet slipped about the stones; so he went on staggering and panting, while the old woman cried from off his back: "Fool, you have wet my mantle! Do you make game of poor old souls like me?"

Jason had half a mind to drop her, and let her get through the torrent by herself; but Cheiron's words were in his mind, and he said only: "Patience, mother; the best horse may stumble some day."

At last he staggered to the shore, and set her down upon the bank; and a strong man he must have been, or that wild water he never would have crossed.

He lay panting awhile upon the bank, and then leapt up to go upon his journey; but he cast one look at the old woman, for he thought, "She should thank me once at least."

And as he looked, she grew fairer than all women, and taller than all men on earth; and her garments shone like the summer sea, and her jewels like the stars of heaven; and she looked down on him, with great soft brown eyes, eyes which filled all the glen with light.

And Jason fell upon his knees, and hid his face between his hands.

And she spoke: "I am the Queen of Olympus, Hera the

wife of Zeus. As thou hast done to me, so will I do to thee. Call on me in the hour of need, and try if the gods can forget."

And when Jason looked up, she rose from off the earth, like a pillar of tall white cloud, and floated away across the mountain peaks, toward Olympus the sacred hill. Then Jason grew light of heart; and he blessed old Cheiron for his wise advice.

Then he went down toward Iolcos, and as he walked he found that he had lost one of his sandals in the flood.

And as he went through the street, the people came out to look at him, so tall and fair was he; but some of the elders whispered together; and at last one of them stopped Jason, and called to him: "Fair lad, who are you, and whence come you; and what is your errand in the town?"

"My name, good father, is Jason, and I come from Pelion up above; and my errand is to Pelias your king. Tell me then where his palace is."

But the old man started, and grew pale, and said: "Do you not know the prophecy, my son, that you go so boldly through the town, with but one sandal on?"

"I am a stranger here, and know of no prophecy; but what of my one sandal?"

Then the old man said: "I will tell you, lest you rush upon your ruin unawares. The oracle in the temple of the gods in Delphi has said that a man wearing one sandal shall take the kingdom from Pelias, and keep it for himself. Therefore beware, for Pelias is the fiercest and most cunning of all kings."

Then Jason laughed a great laugh, like a war horse in his pride—"Good news, good father, both for you and me. For that very end I came into the town."

Then he strode on toward the palace of Pelias, while all the people wondered at his bearing.

And he stood in the doorway and cried: "Come out, Pelias the valiant, and fight for your kingdom like a man."

Pelias came out wondering. "Who are you, bold youth?" he cried.

"I am Jason, the son of Aeson, the heir of all this land."

Then Pelias lifted up his hands and eyes and wept, or seemed to weep; and blessed the heavens which had brought his nephew to him, never to leave him more.

So he drew Jason in, whether he would or not, and spoke to him so lovingly and feasted him so well, that Jason's anger passed.

But after supper Jason said to Pelias: "Why do you look so sad, my uncle? And what did you mean just now, when you said that this was a doleful kingdom, and its ruler a miserable man?"

Then Pelias sighed heavily again and again and again, like a man who had to tell some dreadful story and was afraid to begin. "For seven long years and more have I never known a quiet night; and no more will he who comes after me, till the Golden Fleece be brought to Iolcos."

Now Jason knew of the wonderful Golden Fleece: that it was nailed to a beech tree in the war god's wood in far-off Colchis, realm of King Aietes; and that it was guarded by a sleepless dragon. He also knew that for any mortal man to win the fleece and carry it away was looked on as hopeless and impossible. So he sat silent.

When Pelias saw him silent, he began to talk of other things, and courted Jason more and more, speaking to him as if he was certain to be his heir, and asking his advice about the kingdom; till Jason could not help saying to himself, "Surely he is not the dark man whom people call him. Yet why did he drive my father out?" And he asked Pelias boldly: "Men say that you are terrible, and a man of blood; but I find you a kind and hospitable man. Yet why did you drive my father out?"

Pelias smiled and sighed: "Men have slandered me in that, as in all things. Your father was growing old and weary, and he gave the kingdom up to me of his own will. You shall see him tomorrow, and ask him; and he will tell you the same."

Jason's heart leapt in him, when he heard that he was

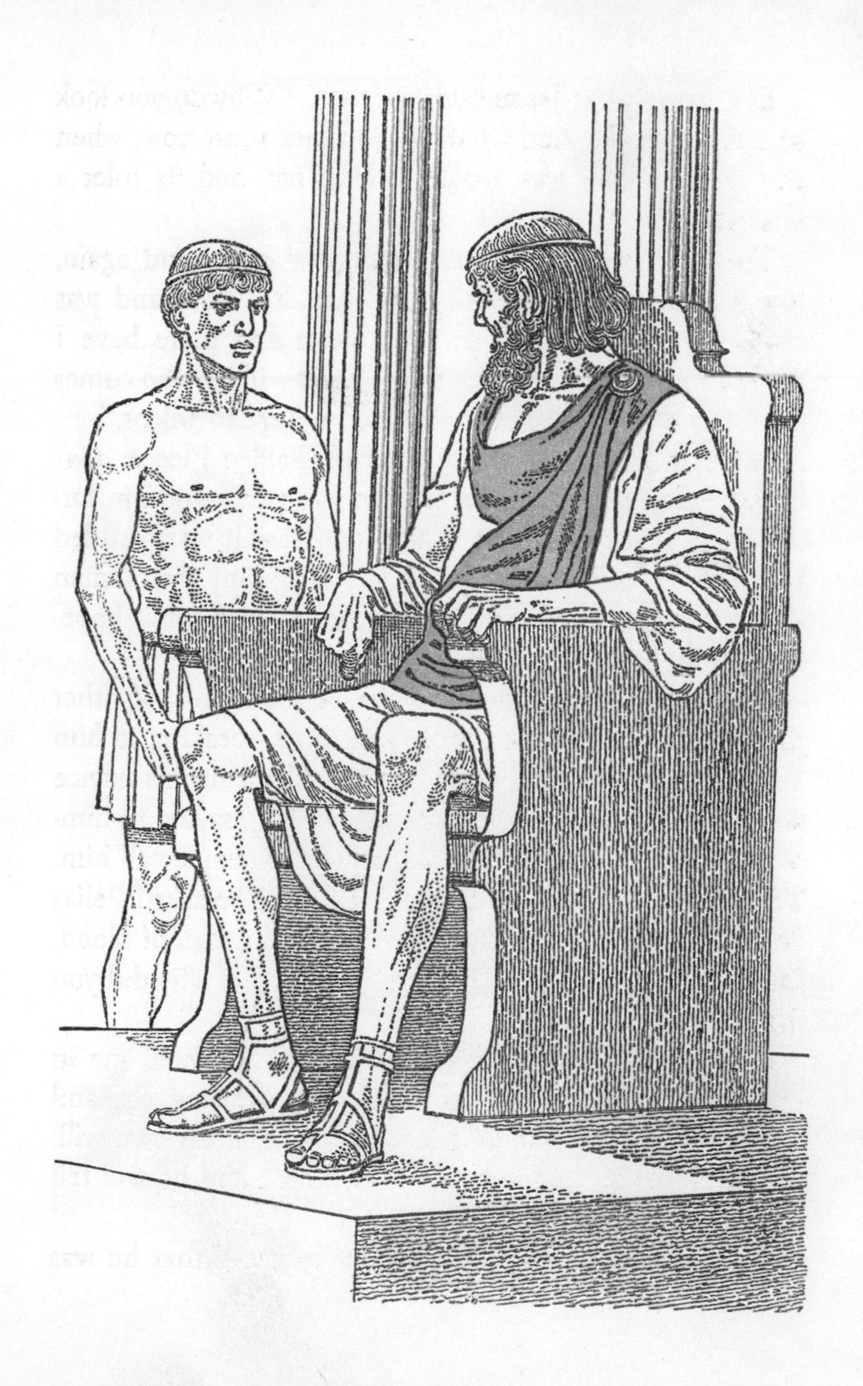

to see his father; and he believed all that Pelias said.

"One thing more there is," said Pelias, "on which I need your advice; for though you are young, I see in you a wisdom beyond your years. There is one neighbour of mine, whom I dread more than all men on earth. I am stronger than he now, and can command him; but I know that if he stay among us, he will work my ruin in the end. Can you give me a plan, Jason, by which I can rid myself of that man?"

After a while, Jason answered, half laughing: "Were I you, I would send him to fetch that same Golden Fleece; for if he once set forth after it you would never be troubled with him more."

At that a bitter smile came across Pelias' lips; and a

flash of wicked joy into his eyes. And he said: "A wise plan, my son. He shall be sent forthwith."

And Jason, seeing the evil in his uncle's face, remembered the warning of the old man; and he cried, starting up:

"You mean me!" And he lifted his fist angrily, while Pelias stood up to face him like a wolf at bay.

Then after a moment crafty Pelias spoke: "Why so rash, my son? You, and not I, have said that my enemy should be sent to fetch the Golden Fleece."

And Jason saw that he was taken in a trap; and he cried:

"You have well spoken, cunning uncle of mine! I love glory, and I dare to keep to my word. I will go and fetch this Golden Fleece. Promise me but this in return, and keep your word as I keep mine. Treat my father lovingly while I am gone, for the sake of the all-seeing Zeus; and give me up the kingdom for my own, on the day that I bring back the Golden Fleece."

Then Pelias looked at him and said: "I promise, and I will perform. It will be no shame to give up my kingdom to the man who wins that fleece."

Then they swore a great oath between them.

And on the morrow Jason went to Pelias, and said: "If you are indeed in earnest, give me two heralds, that they may go round to all the heroes who were pupils of the Centaur with me, that we may fit out a ship together, and take what shall befall."

At that Pelias hastened to send the heralds out; for he said in his heart, "Let all the heroes go with him, and like him, never return; for so I shall be lord of all the land, and the greatest king in Greece."

So the heralds went out, and cried to all the heroes: "Who dare come to the adventure of the Golden Fleece?"

And the goddess Hera stirred all the hearts of the heroes, and they came from all their valleys to the yellow sands of Iolcos. And first came Heracles the mighty, with his lion's skin and club, and Tiphys the skillful steersman; and thither came Ancaios who could read the stars, and Argus, the famed shipbuilder, and many a hero more, in helmets of brass and gold with tall dyed horse-hair crests, and embroidered shirts of linen beneath their coats of mail, and greaves of polished tin to guard their knees in fight; with each man his shield upon his shoulder, of many a fold of tough bull's hide, and his sword of tempered bronze in his silver-studded belt, and in his right hand a pair of lances, of the heavy white ash staves.

So they came down to Iolcos, and all the city came out to meet them, and were never tired with looking at their height, and their beauty, and their gallant bearing, and the glitter of their inlaid arms. And some said, "Never was there such a gathering of the heroes since the Greeks conquered the land."

Then they felled the pines on Pelion, and shaped them with the axe, and Argus taught them to build a galley, the first long ship which ever sailed the seas. They pierced her for fifty oars, an oar for each hero of the crew, and pitched her with coal-black pitch, and painted her bows with vermilion; and they named her Argo after Argus, and worked at her all day long.

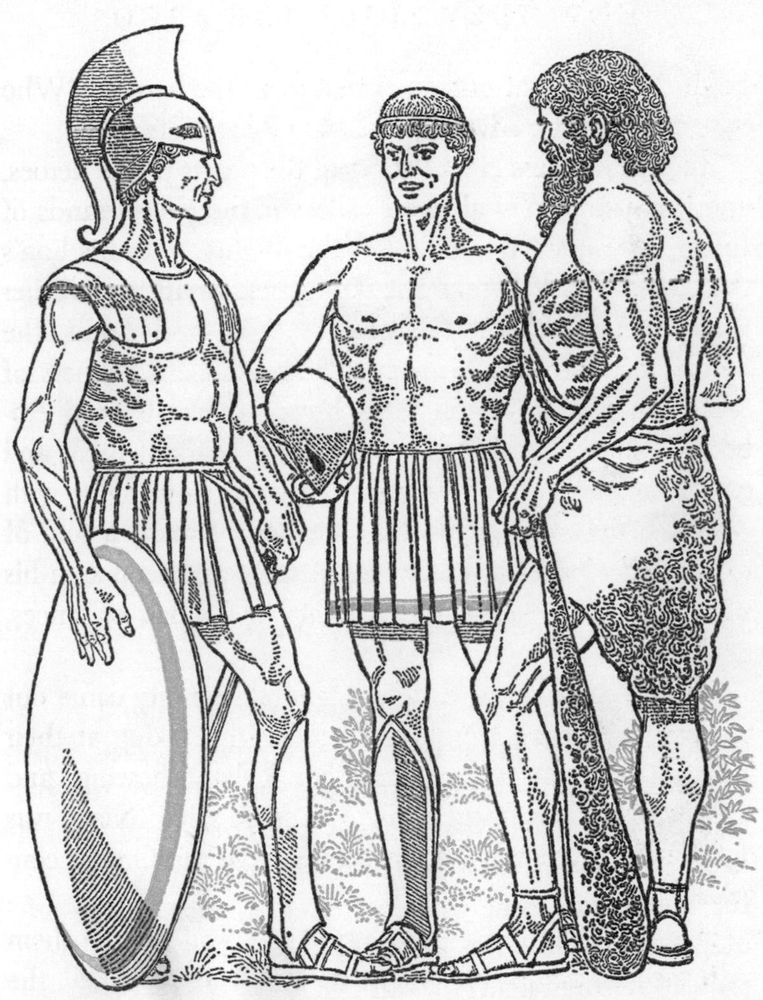

But Jason went away to the northward, and into the land of Thrace, till he found Orpheus the prince of harpists. And he asked him: "Will you leave your mountains, Orpheus, my fellow scholar in old times, to sail with the heroes, and bring home the Golden Fleece, and charm

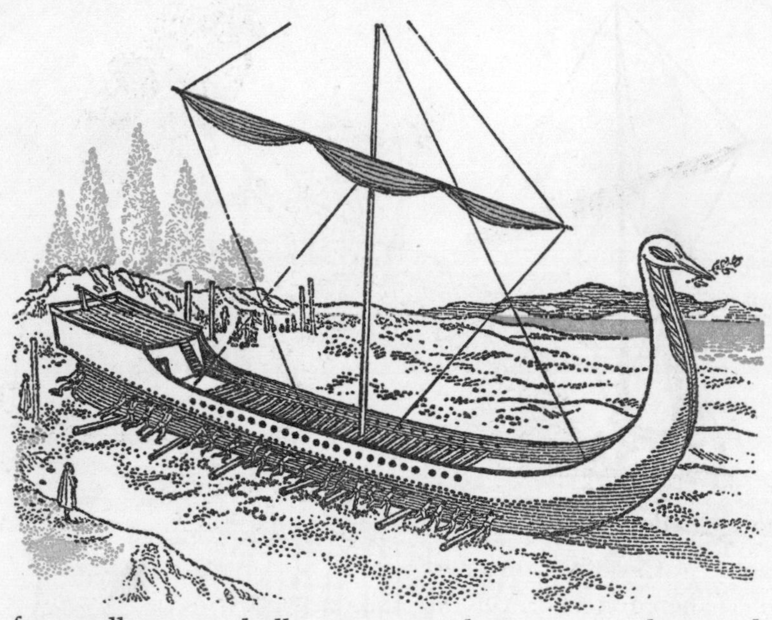

for us all men and all monsters with your magic harp and song?"

Then Orpheus consented, and rose up and took his harp. And he led Jason to the sacred grove of Zeus, where in the darkness of the ancient wood they came to the great oak tree—the magic tree of Zeus and Hera. And Orpheus bade Jason cut down a bough of the oak. Then they took the bough and came to Iolcos, and nailed it to the prow of the ship. Thus the magic of the goddess Hera would protect the Argo henceforward.

And at last the ship was finished, and they tried to launch her down the beach; but she was too heavy for them to move her, and her keel sank deep in the sand. Then Jason spoke, and said: "Let us ask the magic bough; perhaps it can help us in our need."

Then a voice came from the bough, and Jason heard the words it said. And Jason bade Orpheus play upon the harp, while the heroes waited round, holding the pine-trunk rollers, to help her toward the sea.

Then Orpheus took his harp, and began his magic song.

And the good ship Argo stirred in every timber, and heaved from stem to stern, and leapt up from the sand upon the rollers, and plunged onward, till she rushed into the whispering sea.

Then they stored her well with food and water, and pulled the ladder up on board, and settled themselves each man to his oar, and kept time to Orpheus' harp; and away across the bay they rowed southward, while the people lined the cliffs; and the women wept while the men shouted, at the starting of that gallant crew.

HOW THEY SAILED TO COLCHIS

And what happened next, my children, whether it be true or not, stands written in ancient songs, which you shall read for yourselves some day.

The Argonauts sailed away, into unknown eastern seas; and many were the adventures that they encountered before they came at last to Colchis. It is told that they rowed past Olympus, the mountain of the gods; past the wooded bay of Samothrace; through the Hellespont to a doleful isle where they slew the giant, Amycus. They sailed, then, up the Bosporus where the shrieking Harpies—fearful monsters with the faces and hair of fair maidens and the wings and claws of hawks—made battle with the winds until the sea boiled up with foam, and the clouds were dashed against the cliffs. Then into the wild Black Sea they came, to the place of the Clashing Rocks. These terrible rocks shone like spires and castles of grey glass. And as the heroes neared, they could see them heaving, upon the long sea-waves, crashing and grinding together, till the roar went up to heaven. The sea sprang up in spouts between them, and swept round them in white sheets of foam.

The heroes' hearts sank within them, and they lay upon their oars in fear; but Orpheus called to Tiphys the helmsman: "Between them we must pass; so look ahead for an opening, and be brave, for Hera is with us." But Tiphys the helmsman saw a heron come flying mast-high toward the rocks; and he cried: "Hera has sent us a pilot; let us follow the cunning bird."

Then the heron flapped to and fro a moment, till he saw a hidden gap, and into it he rushed like an arrow, while the heroes watched what would befall.

And the blue rocks clashed together as the bird fled swiftly through; but they struck but a feather from his tail, and then rebounded apart.

Then Tiphys cheered the heroes, and they shouted; and the oars bent like withes beneath their strokes, as they rushed between those toppling ice-crags, and the cold blue lips of death. And ere the rocks could meet again they had passed them, and were safe out in the open sea.

And after that they sailed on wearily along the Asian coast.

And they went on past many a mighty river's mouth, and past many a barbarous tribe, till they saw white snow-

peaks hanging, glittering sharp and bright above the clouds. And they knew that they were come to Colchis, at the end of all the earth.

And they rowed three days to the eastward, while Colchis rose higher hour by hour, till they saw—shining above the treetops—the golden roofs of the palace of King Aietes, the child of the Sun.

Then out spoke Tiphys the helmsman: "We are come to our goal at last; for there are the roofs of Aietes, and the woods where all poisons grow; but who can tell us where among them is hid the Golden Fleece? Many a toil must we bear ere we find it, and bring it home to Greece."

But Jason cheered the heroes, for his heart was high and bold; and he said: "I will go alone up to Aietes, though he be the child of the Sun, and win him with soft words.

Better so than to go all together, and to come to blows at once." But the heroes would not stay behind, so they rowed boldly up the stream.

And a dream came to King Aietes, and filled his heart with fear. He thought he saw a shining star, which fell into his daughter's lap; and that Medeia his daughter took it gladly, and carried it to the riverside, and cast it in; and there the whirling river bore it down, and out into the sea.

Then he leapt up in fear, and bade his servants bring his chariot, that he might go down to the riverside. So he went down in his golden chariot, and by his side rode his daughter, Medeia the fair witch-maiden, and behind him a crowd of servants and soldiers, for he was a rich and mighty prince.

And as he drove down by the reedy river, he saw the Argo sliding up beneath the bank, and many a hero in her, like gods for beauty and for strength.

And when they came near together and looked into each other's eyes, the heroes were awed before Aietes as he shone in his chariot, like his father the glorious Sun; for his robes were of rich gold tissue, and the rays of his diadem flashed fire; and in his hand he bore a jewelled sceptre, which glittered like the stars; and sternly he looked at them under his brows, and sternly he spoke, and loud:

"Who are you, and what do you want here, that you come to the shore of Colchis?"

And the heroes sat silent before the face of that ancient king. But the goddess Hera put courage into Jason's heart, and he rose and shouted loudly in answer: "We are no pirates nor lawless men. We come not to plunder and to ravage. Pelias, my uncle, King of Iolcos, has set me on a quest to bring home the Golden Fleece. These, my bold comrades, are heroes far renowned. We know well how to give blows and to take blows; yet we wish to be guests at your table; it will be better so for both."

Then Aietes' rage rushed up like a whirlwind, and his eyes flashed fire as he heard; but he crushed his anger down in his breast, and spoke mildly a cunning speech:

"If you will fight for the fleece with my Colchians, then many a man must die. But do you indeed expect to win from me the fleece in fight? So few against my mighty army? No! If you will be ruled by me, you will find it better far to choose the best man among you, and let him fulfill the labours which I demand. Then I will give him the Golden Fleece for a prize and a glory to you all."

So saying, he turned his horses and drove back in silence to the town. And the heroes sat silent with sorrow; for there was no facing the thousands of the Colchians, and the fearful chance of war.

But Medeia, King Aietes' daughter, thought of Jason and his brave countenance, and said to herself, "If there was one among them who knew no fear, I could show him how to win the fleece."

So in the dusk of evening she went down to the riverside, and crept forward among the beds of reeds, till she came where the heroes were sleeping on the thwarts of the ship, while Jason kept watch on shore, and leant upon his lance full of thought.

Medeia, the fair witch-woman, came to Jason and said: "O brave Jason, go home before you die!"

"It would be base to go home now, fair princess, and to have sailed all these seas in vain."

"But you know not," said Medeia, "what he must do who would win the fleece. He must tame the two brazen-footed bulls, who breathe devouring flame; and with them he must plough, ere nightfall, four acres in the field of Ares; and he must sow them with serpents' teeth, of which each tooth springs up into an armed man. Then he must fight with all those warriors; and little will it profit him to conquer them; for the fleece is guarded by a dragon, more huge than any mountain pine; and over his body you must step, if you would reach the Golden Fleece."

Then Jason laughed bitterly. "Unjustly is that fleece kept here, and by an unjust and lawless king; and unjustly shall I die, for I will attempt it ere another sun be set."

Then Medeia trembled, and said: "No mortal man can reach that fleece, unless I guide him through. For round it, beyond the river, is a wall full nine ells high, with lofty towers and buttresses, and mighty gates of threefold brass."

"No wall so high but it may be climbed at last, and no wood so thick but it may be crawled through; no dragon so wary but he may be charmed, and I may yet win the Golden Fleece, if a wise maiden help bold men."

And he looked at Medeia cunningly, and held her with his glittering eye, till she blushed and trembled, and said: "Who can face the fire of the bulls' breath, and fight ten thousand armed men?"

"He whom you help," said Jason, flattering her, "for your fame is spread over all the earth. Are you not the queen of all enchantresses?"

"Well, if it must be so—for why should you die?—I have an ointment here; I made it from the magic ice-flower. Anoint yourself, your armour, and your weapons with it, and neither fire nor sword can harm you. But what you begin you must end before sunset, for its virtue lasts only one day. And anoint your helmet with it before you sow the serpents' teeth; and when the sons of earth spring up, cast your helmet among their ranks, and the deadly crop of the war god's field will mow itself, and perish."

Then Jason fell on his knees before her, and thanked her; and she gave him the vase of ointment, and fled trembling through the reeds. And Jason told his comrades what had happened, and showed them the box of ointment; and all rejoiced.

And at sunrise Jason went and bathed, and anointed himself from head to foot, and his shield, and his helmet, and his weapons. Then the heroes went up among the marble walls, and beneath the roofs of gold, and stood in Aietes' hall, while he grew pale with rage.

"Fulfill your promise to us, child of the blazing sun. Give us the serpents' teeth, and let loose the fiery bulls; for we have found a champion among us who can win the Golden Fleece."

And Aietes bit his lips, for he fancied that they had fled away by night; but he could not go back from his promise; so he gave them the serpents' teeth.

Then he called for his chariot and his horses, and sent heralds through all the town; and all the people went out with him to the dreadful war god's field.

And there Aietes sat upon his throne, with his warriors

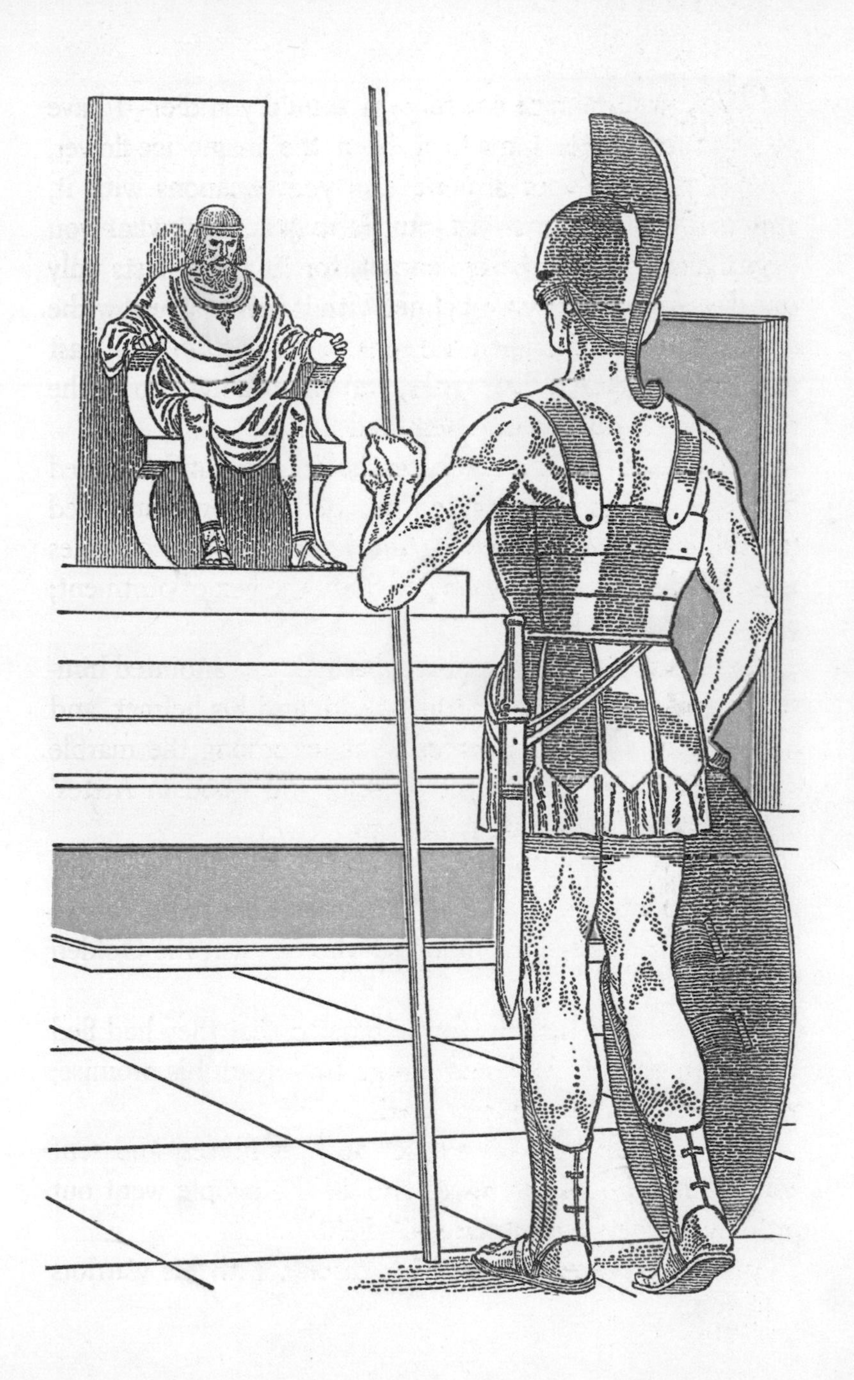

on each hand, thousands and tens of thousands, clothed from head to foot in steel-chain mail. And the people crowded to every window, and bank, and wall; while the heroes stood together, a mere handful in the midst of that great host.

And Medeia was there, wrapped closely in her veil; but Aietes did not know that she was muttering spells between her lips.

Then Jason cried: "Fulfill your promise, and let your fiery bulls come forth."

Then Aietes bade open the gates, and the magic bulls leapt out. Their brazen hoofs rang upon the ground, and their nostrils sent out sheets of flame, as they rushed with lowered heads upon Jason; but he never flinched a step. The flame of their breath swept round him, but it singed not a hair of his head; and the bulls stopped short and trembled, when Medeia began her spell.

Then Jason sprang upon the nearest bull, and seized him by the horns; and up and down they wrestled, till the bull fell grovelling on his knees.

So both the bulls were tamed and yoked; and Jason bound them to the plough, and goaded them onward with his lance, till he had ploughed the sacred field.

And all the heroes shouted; but Aietes bit his lips with rage; for half of Jason's work was over, and the sun was yet high in heaven.

Then he took the serpents' teeth and sowed them, and waited what would befall. But Medeia looked at him and at his helmet, lest he should forget the lesson she had taught.

And every furrow heaved and bubbled, and out of every

clod rose a man. Out of the earth they rose by thousands, each clad from head to foot in steel, and drew their swords and rushed on Jason, where he stood in the midst alone.

Then the heroes grew pale with fear for him; and Aietes laughed a bitter laugh.

But Jason snatched off his helmet, and hurled it into the thickest of the throng. And blind madness came upon them, suspicion, hate, and fear; and one cried to his fellow: "Thou didst strike me!" and another: "Thou art Jason; thou shalt die!" So fury seized those earth-born phantoms, and each turned his hand against the rest; and they fought and were never weary, till they all lay dead upon the ground. Then the magic furrows opened, and the kind earth took them home into her breast; and the grass grew up again above them, and Jason's work was done.

Then the heroes rose and shouted, and Jason cried: "Lead me to the fleece this moment, before the sun goes down."

But Aietes thought, "He has conquered the bulls; and reaped the deadly crop. He may kill the dragon yet." So he delayed, and sat taking counsel with his princes, till the sun went down and all was dark. Then he bade a herald cry: "Every man to his home for tonight. Tomorrow we will meet these heroes, and speak about the Golden Fleece."

Then he turned and looked at Medeia: "This is your doing, false witch-maid! You have helped these yellow-haired strangers, and brought shame upon your father and yourself!"

Medeia shrank and trembled, and her face grew pale with fear; and Aietes knew that she was guilty, and whispered: "If they win the fleece, you die!"

But the heroes marched toward their ship, growling like lions cheated of their prey; for they saw that Aietes meant to mock them, and cheat them out of all their toil.

And after a while Medeia came trembling, and wept a long while before she spoke: "My end is come, and I must die; for my father has found out that I have helped you. You he would kill if he dared; but he will not harm you, because you have been his guests. Go then, go, and remember poor Medeia when you are far across the sea."

But all the heroes cried: "If you die, we die with you; for without you we cannot win the fleece, and home we will not go without it, but fall here fighting to the last man."

"You need not die," said Jason. "Flee home with us across the sea. Show us but how to win the fleece, and come with us, and you shall be my queen, and rule over the rich princes, in Iolcos by the sea."

And all the heroes pressed round, and vowed to her that she should be their queen.

Medeia wept, and hid her face in her hands; but at last she looked up at Jason, and spoke between her sobs: "Must I leave my home and my people, to wander with strangers across the sea? The lot is cast, and I must endure it. I will show you how to win the Golden Fleece. Bring up your ship to the woodside, and moor her there against the bank; and let Jason come up at midnight, and one brave comrade with him, and meet me beneath the wall."

Then all the heroes cried together: "I will go!" "And I!" "And I!" But Medeia calmed them, and said: "Orpheus shall go with Jason, and bring his magic harp; for I hear that he is the king of all minstrels, and can charm all things on earth."

And Orpheus laughed for joy, because the choice had fallen on him.

So at midnight they went up the bank, and found Medeia.

Medeia brought them to a thicket, beside the war god's gate; and the bars of the gates fell down, and the brazen doors flew wide. Then Medeia and the heroes ran forward and hurried through the poison wood, among the dark stems of the mighty beeches, guided by the gleam of the Golden Fleece, until they saw it hanging on one vast tree in the midst. And Jason would have sprung to seize it; but Medeia held him back, and pointed shuddering to the tree foot, where the mighty dragon lay, coiled in and out among the roots, with a body like a mountain pine. His coils stretched many a fathom, spangled with bronze and gold; and half of him they could see, but no more; for the rest lay in the darkness far beyond.

And when he saw them coming, he lifted up his head, and watched them with his small bright eyes, and flashed his forked tongue, and roared like the fire among the woodlands, till the forest tossed and groaned.

But Medeia called gently to him; and he stretched out his long spotted neck, and licked her hand, and looked up in her face, as if to ask for food. Then she made a sign to Orpheus, and he began his magic song.

And as he sang, the forest grew calm again, and the leaves on every tree hung still; and the dragon's head sank down, and his brazen coils grew limp, and his glittering eyes closed lazily, till he breathed as gently as a child.

Then Jason leapt forward warily, and stepped across that

mighty monster, and tore the fleece from off the tree trunk; and the three rushed down the garden, to the bank where the Argo lay.

There was a silence for a moment, while Jason held the Golden Fleece on high. Then he cried: "Go now, good Argo, swift and steady, if ever you would see the land of Greece again."

And the great ship went, as the heroes drove her, grim and silent all, with muffled oars, till the pine wood bent like willow in their hands, and stout Argo groaned beneath their strokes.

On and on, beneath the dewy darkness, they fled

swiftly down the swirling stream; underneath black walls, and temples, and the castles of the princes of the East; past fragrant gardens, and groves of all strange fruits; past marshes and long beds of whispering reeds; till they heard the merry music of the surf as it tumbled on the bar.

Into the surf they rushed, and the Argo leapt the breakers like a horse, till the heroes stopped, all panting, each man upon his oar, as she slid into the still broad sea.

Then Orpheus took his harp and sang a song of triumph and joy, till the heroes' hearts rose high again; and they rowed on stoutly and steadfastly, away into the darkness of the West.

So they fled away to the westland; and a dark journey lay before them, and years of bitter toil. For out of the heavens came a storm that swept the Argo far from her course, into the wastes of a wild wide western sea. Whither they wandered in this unknown sea I cannot tell. The old songs speak of Aiaia, the fairy island of the West—and is this the Azores? Some say they came to a place where they had to drag their ship across the land nine days with ropes and rollers—was this in Africa? But all say they came at last to the pillars of Hercules and the Mediterranean Sea. Thence they sailed on, past the Tyrrhenian shore, till they came to a flowery island, upon a still bright summer's eve. And as they neared it slowly and wearily, they heard sweet songs upon the shore. But when Medeia heard the songs, she started, and cried: "Beware, all heroes, for these are the rocks of the Sirens. You must pass close by them, for there is no other channel; but those who listen to that song are lost."

Then spoke Orpheus, the king of all minstrels: "Let them match their song against mine. I have charmed stones, and trees, and dragons, how much more the hearts of men!" So he caught up his lyre, and stood upon the deck, and began his magic song.

And now they could see the Sirens, on the flowery isle: three fair maidens sitting on the beach, beneath a red rock in the setting sun, among beds of crimson poppies and golden asphodel. Slowly they sang and sleepily, with silver voices, mild and clear, which stole over the golden waters,

and into the hearts of all the heroes, in spite of Orpheus' song.

And as the heroes listened, the oars fell from their hands, and their heads drooped on their breasts, and they closed their heavy eyes; and they dreamed of bright still gardens, and of slumbers under murmuring pines, till all their toil seemed foolishness, and they thought of their renown no more.

Then one lifted his head suddenly, and cried: "What use in wandering forever? Let us stay here and rest awhile." And another: "Let us row to the shore, and hear the words they sing."

Then Medeia clapped her hands together, and cried: "Sing louder, Orpheus, sing a bolder strain; wake up these hapless sluggards, or none of them will see the land of Greece again."

Then Orpheus lifted his harp, and crashed his cunning hand across the strings; and his music and his voice rose like a trumpet through the still evening air; into the air it rushed like thunder, till the rocks rang and the sea; and into their souls it rushed like wine, till all hearts beat fast within their breasts.

And he sang the song of Perseus, how the gods led him over land and sea, and how he slew the loathly Gorgon, and how he sits now with the gods upon Olympus, honoured by all men below.

So Orpheus sang, and the Sirens sang, answering each other across the golden sea, till Orpheus' voice drowned the Sirens, and the heroes caught their oars again.

And they cried: "We will be men like Perseus, and we will dare and suffer to the last. Sing us his song again, brave Orpheus, that we may forget the Sirens and their spell."

And as Orpheus sang, they dashed their oars into the sea, and kept time to his music, as they fled fast away; and the Sirens' voices died behind them, in the hissing of the foam along their wake.

After that they rowed on steadily for many a weary day, till—after many more adventures—they came, all worn and tired, to Iolcos by the sea.

And they ran the ship ashore; but they had no strength left to haul her up the beach; and they crawled out on the pebbles, and sat down, and wept till they could weep no more. For the houses and the trees were all altered; and all the faces which they saw were strange; and their joy was swallowed up in sorrow, while they thought of their youth, and all their labour, and their long, long wandering.

And the people crowded round, and asked them: "Who are you, that you sit weeping here?"

"We are the sons who sailed out many a year ago. We went to fetch the Golden Fleece; and we have brought it. Give us news of our fathers and our mothers, if any of them be left alive on earth."

Then there was shouting and laughing, and weeping; and all the people came to the shore, and they led away the heroes to their homes.

Then Jason went up with Medeia to the palace of his uncle Pelias. And when he came in, Pelias sat by the hearth, bent with age; while opposite him sat Aeson, Jason's father, bent likewise; and the two old men's heads shook together, as they tried to warm themselves before the fire.

And Jason fell down at his father's knees, and wept, and called him by his name. And the old man stretched his hands out, and felt him, and said: "Do not mock me, young hero. My son Jason is dead long ago at sea."

"I am your own son Jason, whom you trusted to the Centaur upon Pelion; and I have brought home the Golden Fleece, and a princess of the Sun for my bride."

Then his father clung to him like a child, and wept, and would not let him go; and cried: "Promise me never to leave me while I live."

And Jason promised. Then he turned to King Pelias and said: "Now give me up the kingdom, my uncle, and fulfill your vow as I have fulfilled mine."

So Pelias was king no more; and Jason ruled long and wisely in Iolcos by the sea.

Gregorio and the White Llama

by LAURA BANNON

illustrated by DOBRI

High up in the mountains of Peru there is a land of clouds and rocks and grass and big cactus plants with red flowers. There, on the very top of the world, sat a little Indian boy. His name was Gregorio Condori.

He was a very lucky boy because his father owned a herd or train of llamas. But he didn't feel lucky at all.

More than anything else in the whole world, Gregorio wanted to drive the llama train all by himself. But every time he coaxed to do it, his father answered just like fathers everywhere.

He said, "When you are older."

Lately Father had sometimes been saying, "When you are more responsible."

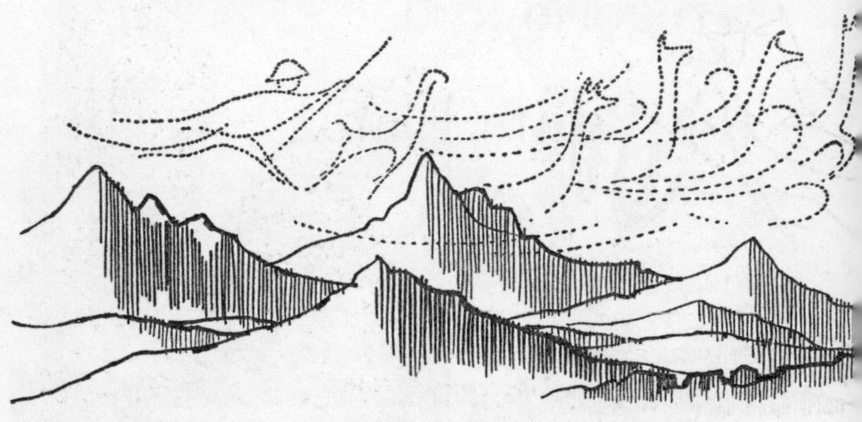

Gregorio knew, all right, just what Father meant by that.

It was Gregorio's job to keep a close watch over the llamas while they fed on the coarse ychu grass in the rocky pasture. But even though he liked the llamas very much, he got tired of watching them all day as they grazed.

His big trouble was that sometimes, when the afternoon sun warmed the chilly air, he would fall asleep in spite of himself. Then the llamas would wander away out of sight.

He knew this was not the way to be more responsible. He also knew that if he couldn't prove to his father that he was more responsible, he would never be able to drive the llama train.

Gregorio sat on the big rock with his arms around his knees and his feet tucked under his poncho. He opened his eyes extra wide just to be sure he was not falling asleep as he watched the llamas grazing near the rock.

They were all fine llamas, but the big white one was the pride of the Condori family. He was the leader, and besides being beautiful he was especially smart.

Gregorio couldn't imagine doing anything more thrilling than driving a llama train with this wonderful white leader at the head. It would be easy to do, he thought. Easier than watching them all day in the pasture without falling asleep.

A rooster crowed on the opposite mountain. Then the Cathedral bells rang in the village down the cliff almost straight below the pasture. The sky was as blue as anything. Gregorio watched the gray and white clouds streak across the snow-covered peaks like a swift train of llamas. He grew drowsy as he watched them, and soon he fell asleep.

He dreamed he was driving the cloud llamas. He raced after them, calling out to the white leader in a deep voice like Father's, "*Vamos!* Hurry, white one! On with you!"

Faster and faster they sped and soon they reached the narrow streets of the village below. A man called out, "What will you take for the white one, Señor?"

Gregorio patted the money bag at his belt and called back, "Money cannot buy him."

The sun sank behind a mountain peak and Gregorio kept on dreaming, all hunched up under his poncho, with his head on his knees.

In a little straw-covered hut in the distance, Gregorio's mother was starting the supper. She had built a fire on the raised fireplace in the middle of the hard earth floor. Smoke from the fire curled out the open door of the hut. Here sister Clotilde was playing with Bcbccito, thc baby brother.

Father Condori came up to the hut with a pile of empty sacks on his back. He stood the sacks inside the doorway and said, "Has Gregorio brought in the llamas yet?"

As he said it he squinted his eyes and looked out at the pasture land. It didn't take Father long to understand the meaning of the bump he saw on the big rock.

"The boy has gone to sleep again!" exclaimed Father angrily. He stalked across the pasture calling "Gregorio! Gregorio!"

Gregorio woke with a sudden start. Father was right beside him, calling his name, and the llamas were nowhere in sight.

Oh! Oh! He had done it again!

"A fine son I have," said Father. "Every day you ask to drive the llama train. Yet you cannot be trusted to watch the beasts in the pasture. Perhaps this time you have really lost them."

Gregorio was scared. He ran quickly with Father to a rise in the land and peered into the dusky gully below. Father heaved a big sigh of relief. The llamas were there grazing peacefully.

Father drove them back to the pen built against the side of the hut.

"How do you think we would get the sacks of grain to the mill tomorrow if the llamas were lost?" scolded Father.

The next day Gregorio and Mother helped Father fill the grain sacks. And Clotilde watched Bebecito and shooed the chickens out of the grain.

The sacks were all exactly the right size. For if too many pounds are put on a llama's back, he will lie down and he won't get up until they are taken off.

Gregorio thought this was very strange. Father and Mother often carried huge loads. On the mountain paths and in the market places, Indians could be seen everywhere carrying such things on their backs as sewing machines and pigs, and jars so big that a man could crawl into one of them.

Neighbor Quispe's little burro didn't complain when she put a load of grass on his back and then climbed on top with the baby. But everyone knew that they couldn't do that to a llama.

When all the sacks were filled and loaded on the llamas' backs, Mother tied Bebecito in her carrying-shawl.

Father called out, "*Vamos!* We are on our way."

The white llama started off down the trail from the hut and the family trotted along behind. They zigzagged back and forth past big clumps of cacti. Pretty soon they were in the village streets.

When they came to the big plaza, the white llama stopped at the little hat shop on the corner. He stood and

gazed at the windows.

"*Vamos!*" shouted everyone. "On with you!"

Father and Mother and Gregorio pushed and pulled and coaxed. The llamas blocked the street. Automobile horns honked. The drivers shook their fists and shouted, "Clear the way!"

But people, burros, automobiles, and push carts had to wait until the white llama was ready to move on.

He liked the shiny glass windows filled with rows of colored straw hats and he always stopped for a while to look at them.

When they got started again, the llama train passed the big Cathedral with its dark red doors. Then it turned into the courtyard of the mill where the llamas were unloaded. They chewed their cuds while they waited.

Gregorio and Clotilde liked the mill room. Fine white flour flew through the air. The mill room floor was always powdered with it. It puffed up between toes and was carried in long ghost tracks across the courtyard by the soles of bare feet.

Today an artist was sitting at the end of the courtyard sketching the llamas. Now he started walking around the white llama while he sketched him.

Gregorio and Clotilde stood on tiptoe to see the drawings on his pad, and this is what they saw.

The artist sketched a back view, front view and three-quarter view. Then he squatted on the ground, squinted his eyes, and looking up under the white llama's chin, he sketched him from that angle.

As Father and Mother Condori came up, the artist took

his pipe out of his mouth and made a little speech to Father.

"You have a very fine llama. I would like your permission to have him pose for a statue I am to make. I will pay you well if you will let the children bring him to my studio each morning at ten o'clock, beginning two days from now."

Gregorio was all ears as he listened to the artist talk. Now his heart turned a big somersault and then sat very still, listening for Father's answer. To drive the llama to the village and watch the artist make a statue would be a wonderful and important event.

"We are honored to have the llama pose, Señor," said Father. "I will see that he gets to your studio at the proper time."

Gregorio's heart fell *ker-plop* to the bottom of his stomach. He knew Father was remembering that he had fallen asleep again while he watched the llamas. Oh, why had he done it?

"The sun is low. We must be on our way," said Father. Mother hitched Bebecito higher on her back and tightened the knot in her shawl.

Vamos! The white llama started off down the street followed by the rest of the train.

A woman with a candy stand called out, "Sweets for small pennies," and Father bought some candied oranges in a pretty striped sack. They nibbled at the oranges as they trotted along under the little balconies that hung over the street. Then up the mountain trail they went.

Father took a shepherd's pipe from his belt and played a little tune upon it. Gregorio and Clotilde sang the words:

"Up and down the mountain,
Here and there we go;
A mountain with its feet in sand,
Its head up in the snow."

The mountain picked up the sweet music and tossed it across to another mountain. Fainter and fainter it became until Father had to start it all over again on his pipe.

The blue of the sky grew very deep. Indian families were building fires to cook their suppers. The lights twinkled on, like stars against the dark mountains. The white leader was a light spot, moving up a trail that was so steep it seemed to lead straight into the sky. The others followed single file.

When Gregorio lay down on his straw bed that night, wrapped snugly in a wool blanket, he thought about his big trouble. If he could prove he was more responsible, perhaps Father would still let him drive the white llama to the artist's studio.

He thought and thought. Finally he had a plan. Then he

fell asleep.

The next day Gregorio filled the striped candy sack with yarn and took it to the pasture with him. As soon as the llamas began to graze, he found some straight dry stalks and climbed upon the big rock.

Keeping one eye on the llamas, he tied the stalks together in a little frame and slipped the sack over it. Then he fastened a long string tail to that, and tied twigs onto the tail.

The first time he tried to fly the little kite, it took a nose dive. The tail was too light! He tied on more twigs. Now it staggered along close above the rocks. The tail was too heavy! Gregorio was so busy that it wasn't hard at all to stay awake.

When the little kite finally sailed high in the air, Gregorio noticed the white clouds that rode over the towering mountain peaks. Now they seemed to grow tired and were sitting down to rest on the mountain side. He watched them sprawl out and roll down the mountain, swallowing up everything they came to. Soon they would settle in the pasture and hide the llamas from sight.

Quickly Gregorio pulled in the kite. Picking up a big stick, he ran around the llamas to herd them together. Then he shouted at the white one, to start him off toward the hut.

Father Condori was coming in from the grain field. "That was a wise thing to do, Gregorio," he said.

"Am I more responsible?" asked Gregorio.

Father cleared his throat: "Yes, my son. I have decided that you and Clotilde may take the white llama to the artist's studio tomorrow."

"Oh! A thousand thanks, Father. The white one will be

safe, you'll see." He ran into the hut to tell Clotilde about it.

Gregorio was up before the sun the next morning. He crept quietly out the door of the hut to take a look at the white llama.

The black night was just uncovering a world all white with frost. It was icy cold. But that didn't bother the llamas. They had great heavy coats to keep them warm.

Gregorio picked grass out of the white llama's coat and brushed his fleece until it was clean and fluffy. Just to make him look prettier, he placed a string of silver bells around his neck. On the white llama's back, Gregorio tied a little make-believe sack, the kind that llamas wear when they are dressed up for a fiesta.

After a quick breakfast of hot porridge, Clotilde and Gregorio were ready to start to the artist's studio.

"We go!" called Gregorio.

"Remember to keep to the left if you meet an automobile," warned Father. "And the Saints be with you."

The white llama was off down the trail. As he swung his long neck back and forth the bells rang merrily. His spirits were as light as his load.

"Not so fast, white one," called Gregorio. "You will fall off the mountain ledge."

"He thinks he has wings like the vultures and can fly to the Cathedral dome," laughed Clotilde, who was running along behind as fast as her short legs would carry her.

When they reached the village, it was safer to go more slowly. The shopkeepers, opening their stalls along the

street, stopped to watch the white llama pass.

How wonderful to drive such a beautiful animal, thought Gregorio.

But at the hat shop the llama stopped as usual.

"Come on, be a good llama," coaxed Gregorio and Clotilde. "You will make us all late to the artist's studio."

"Maybe he likes to look at the rows of colored hats, the way we like to look at the rows of frosted cakes in the bakery windows," said Clotilde.

"They are made of straw that is like the grass he eats," said Gregorio. "Come on, foolish one, they would make you sick if you ate them."

But the white llama braced his legs when they pushed him. He gazed at the window undisturbed until he was ready to leave. Then they headed him off down the street.

At the studio they found the artist ready to start working. With a heavy wire he had made a little skeleton that was something like the shape of a llama.

"This will be the bones for my clay llama," he said. "It will keep the clay from sagging into a lump."

He posed the Condori llama in a sunny spot in the courtyard and then began packing wet clay around the little skeleton.

Gregorio and Clotilde stood so still against the whitewashed wall of the courtyard that they looked like pictures painted there. Their eyes followed every move the artist made.

People passing in the street stopped in the doorway to watch. They gazed in wonder at the clay that grew slowly, under the artist's hands, into a body with legs and a neck and a head.

They looked at the white llama and said, "What an excellent model he makes."

The Condori llama was indeed an excellent model. Usually when models pose they grow tired and their heads droop forward.

The artist is forever having to say, "Will you lift your chin a little, please? A little more—no, that is too much. There! That is just right, thank you."

This was not necessary with the Condori llama. He held his head high. But sometimes a lump could be seen traveling up his long neck to his mouth. Then he would begin chewing his cud, swinging his lower jaw from side to side. This was a specially good time to get that grass chewed that he had stored away in one of his four extra stomachs.

Day after day the white llama posed. And the clay llama grew more and more complete. It was wonderful! The dull, heavy clay from the bucket had become a spirited little animal.

Somehow it was more than just a statue of the white llama. The onlookers' faces were full of pride as they thought, "There is no other creature so noble-looking as the llama of Peru."

At the end of the week the artist said, "It will not be necessary for your llama to pose again. Here is the money for your father; and here is some for the two of you to spend as you like." He handed Gregorio a handful of bright coins.

Gregorio counted the coins eagerly. There were fifty centavos.

What a lot of money! This was as much as Father could

earn in a long day. Gregorio felt that it must be spent for something very special. He tied the money in the corner of his woolen poncho. Then he and Clotilde hurried home,

eager to show it to Father and Mother.

"You have done well, my son," said Father, "and I am proud of you."

During the week that the white llama posed for the artist, Father and Mother had worked from early morning until sunset threshing out more grain. Now it was tied in sacks and ready to be carried to the mill.

Gregorio was helping to load the sacks on the llamas' backs. Father Condori placed a sack on the white llama's back and was starting to tie it when suddenly the white llama flipped back his ears and plopped himself on the ground, grumbling.

What was wrong here? This sack was of the proper size. Perhaps the white llama had carried the fancy little make-believe sack so long that he could not judge the weight of a decent sack of grain.

Father Condori took it off his back and waited for him to get up. Then he put the sack on again.

Now the white llama shocked everyone. Wheeling around, he glared at Father, his eyes sharp with anger. He pulled his head back for a better aim, and spat straight into Father Condori's face.

Clotilde's and Gregorio's eyes and mouths were round with surprise.

"So! Ho!" roared Father, just as angrily. "So! We shall see! Now you are worth only the wool on your lazy back."

The other llamas were soon loaded and Father drove them down to the mill with the brown llama in the lead. The white llama was left alone in the pasture in disgrace.

Gregorio stayed at home to watch the white llama. How sad, he thought! Nothing could ever come out quite right now, no matter how old or how responsible he might grow to be.

Maybe some day Father would let him drive the llama train by himself. But it wouldn't be half so exciting without the white leader.

The white llama was unhappy too. He didn't eat and he didn't chew his cud. He just stood looking down the trail toward the village. When a fog settled like a ceiling over the pasture Gregorio put him in the pen.

It was late when Father Condori came home with the llamas. In the fog the brown llama had taken the train down the wrong trail at each turn. Father was scratched by thorns and very tired.

Father Condori went out to the llama pen the next morning. With big shears he cut off the white llama's thick coat of wool.

"Should such a back be beautiful? No!" said Father. "This wool will make a fine covering for the backs of those who earn their daily meal."

The white llama looked so funny without his wool that Father had to laugh. His legs were too thin. His joints were too big, and his neck was, oh, so skinny! With the shearing all his grace and dignity seemed to have left him.

The poor creature put back his ears and lay down, complaining mournfully. A cool breeze from the mountain glaciers made him shiver. He felt very sad and gloomy.

As Mother Condori was coloring the white llama's wool with dye, she said again and again, "It will be a pleasure

to make things from this lovely wool. It takes the bright colors so well."

When the wool was dry, she spun it into yarn. Then for Father she made a cap designed with rows of little people and trees.

She crocheted a pair of dolls for Clotilde and a pretty new bonnet with ruffles for Bebecito.

For Gregorio, she knit a beautiful money bag, just like Father's. Now he wouldn't have to tie the coins in the corner of his poncho.

Because there was some wool left, she made a little llama just for fun and trimmed it as for a fiesta.

While Mother Condori was working miracles with the wool, the white llama was growing a thick new coat.

Gregorio kept a close watch over the llamas in the pasture. At the same time he was very busy. He combed wool for Mother and he made a reed pipe and learned to play a little tune upon it.

As the summer passed the grain grew tall in the fields. Then it turned yellow and had to be threshed.

"This is the heaviest crop of grain we have ever had," said Father, happily. "The llamas will never be able to carry it to the mill in one trip."

"Oh, Father!" cried Gregorio, "why couldn't Clotilde and I drive the train to the mill with the first load tomorrow? You and Mother could be finishing the threshing."

"With the brown llama for a leader it would be unwise," said Father. "He has a head of stone."

"If the day is clear the brown llama would know his

way," coaxed Gregorio. "We would hurry home before the clouds settle."

"We would hurry home," echoed Clotilde in a pleading voice that would be hard for any father to refuse.

"W-e-l-l," said Father, considering. "We shall see what the morning is like. Perhaps you may if the day is clear."

The sun rose into a clear sky the next day. So the llamas were carefully loaded for the trip.

"Bring back a sack of flour from the mill," said Father. "And remember to keep your voice low when you talk to the llamas. Be home as early as possible. And don't get excited if the llamas give you trouble."

Gregorio was already excited. Little thrills were chasing up and down his spine, and he felt as if he had no stomach.

"Don't worry, Father. We'll be back soon after the noon

bells ring," he promised as he fastened his new money bag to his belt.

Mother pinned Clotilde's shawl with a cactus thorn. "You can be a big help to Gregorio if the brown llama wants to go down the wrong street," she told Clotilde.

But the brown llama did not go down the wrong street. Gregorio drove the train like a grownup. He had no trouble at all guiding the animals into the courtyard of the mill. It was such fun to drive the train! If only the white llama could have been leader, everything would have been perfect.

The miller came to the door of the mill room. His face and arms were covered with flour and he wore a big smile. "So!" he said, "I see your father now has a man to drive the llamas for him."

Gregorio felt pleased. He helped the miller unload the sacks and carry them into the mill room. When he brought out the sack of flour to take home, Clotilde spoke to her brother in a low, excited voice:

"Look, Gregorio! Look!"

Their eyes popped in amazement, for, stepping neatly over the high sill to the courtyard was their beautiful white llama! He walked over to the llama train and stood calmly with his nose in the air.

"He has come by himself!" whispered Gregorio.

Gregorio carried the sack of flour over to the white llama.

"Nice boy, nice boy!" he said, patting him while he fastened the sack of flour on his back. Then, in a deep voice like Father's he called out: "*Vamos*, my white one!"

With great importance the white llama pushed his way past the other llamas and stepped into the street. First the brown llama and then the others followed obediently.

When they came to the big plaza both Gregorio and Clotilde laughed aloud.

"Our white leader forgets nothing," chuckled Gregorio. "He has stopped at the hat shop again."

There in the window of the hat shop was a delicious-looking new hat—a grass-green straw with raspberry pink trimmings. The white leader stared at it.

"Perhaps he really wants to wear the hat, not eat it," said Clotilde. "You know some of the leaders at the fiesta parade wear little caps on their heads."

"How much is the green hat, Señor?" called Gregorio. The shopkeeper was sitting on the high counter inside his shop. Only his feet and the legs of his checked trousers could be seen through the doorway. Now the feet slid slowly to the floor and his head appeared.

"The green hat is very new," said the shopkeeper. "It has just come from the big city of Lima. Many people will want to buy it, but I will sell it to you for seventy-five centavos."

"That is too much for one small hat that is not long for wear," said Gregorio. "You would do well to part with it for thirty-five centavos before it grows old in the shop."

"No, no! You joke," wailed the shopkeeper. "I cannot live and sell my hats for thirty-five centavos."

"That is unfortunate, Señor. Good day," said Gregorio. "*Vamos!*" he shouted at the white leader, who kept right on gazing at the hat.

"One moment, my young man," said the shopkeeper. "You are my first customer today and so if you will pay me fifty centavos I will make you a present of the hat."

Clotilde watched her brother with admiring eyes. He took the fifty centavos out of his new money bag and handed it to the shopkeeper.

Carefully they cut slits in the brim of the green and pink hat for the white llama's ears, and tied it on his handsome head.

"See, my fine fellow," said Gregorio to the white llama. "You wear a hat prettier than any of the caps of the leader llamas in the fiesta. You are the finest leader in the whole of Peru!"

Now the white llama started down the street toward home. He held his nose high in the air and turned his head slowly from side to side as he watched the sights from under the brim of his hat.

Suddenly there was a loud clanging of bells that scared all the vultures off the Cathedral dome.

"Hurry, my white one!" called the proud llama driver. "The Cathedral bells are ringing. We must be home soon!"

At the head of the trail near the Condori hut stood Father. He had just discovered that the white llama had broken loose from his pen. He was worried.

Around the turn in the trail came the Condori llama train, and in the lead was the dignified white llama with the pretty straw hat resting a little over one eye.

Father put his hands on his hips and, leaning back, roared with laughter. Mother heard the uproar and come running. She laughed until tears came to her eyes. Everyone laughed and laughed.

"Isn't it good, Father, to have our white leader again?" asked Gregorio.

Father put his arm around Gregorio's shoulder and said, "Yes, Gregorio, and it is also good to have a big son I can depend upon to help me in the busy season."

The

Skipping Rope

by ROSE FYLEMAN

illustrated by HARVEY WEISS

There was once a little girl who had a magic skipping rope given to her.

It was a wonderful rope. You took hold of the handles, which were bright red and green, with little bells on them, and you said:

> *"Standing's dull and walking's slow,*
> *Skipping's best—and off we go!"*

And then you did go off.

You just kept on skipping and skipping. The rope turned by itself; you only had to hold the handles, and it never caught in your feet or in your clothes. It always went on, and you went on too.

When you'd had enough you said:

> *"Stop, stop, skipping rope do,*
> *That's enough for me and you."*

And then it stopped.

And one day the little girl forgot the rhyme that made it stop. I think the skipping rope must have got annoyed about something. I'm sure it could have stopped if it had tried.

The little girl's father came and tried to take the rope away when he saw what had happened, but the strange thing was that, as soon as he touched his little girl, he began skipping too, jumping up and down, though he had no rope. His wife came and took hold of him, and she immediately started also; so did the servant, who tried to stop her mistress; so did their little dog, which jumped up at them. There they all were, bobbing up and down and

looking very foolish indeed.

They might have been skipping to this day had not a friend come in. The friend happened to be a poet.

"We've forgotten the rhyme that makes the skipping rope stop," gasped out the father.

"I'll make another for you," said the poet. "One rhyme's as good as another, and better."

And this is the rhyme *he* made:

> *"Stop your tricks and off you pack,*
> *Run away and don't come back."*

The skipping rope stopped at once, but only for a minute.

It jerked itself out of the little girl's hand as if it were in a rage, and then started off again. It skipped down the stairs and out of the house and down the street and out of sight. They didn't try to stop it. They were thankful to be rid of it.

But now you see how useful it is to have a poet for a friend!

A Frog He Would A-Wooing Go

illustrated by ADRIENNE ADAMS

A frog he would a-wooing go,
  Heigh ho! says Rowley,
A frog he would a-wooing go,
Whether his mother would let him or no.
  With a rowley, powley, gammon and spinach,
  Heigh ho! says Anthony Rowley.

So off he set with his opera hat,
Heigh ho! says Rowley,
So off he set with his opera hat,
And on the road he met with a rat.
With a rowley, powley, gammon and spinach,
Heigh ho! says Anthony Rowley.

"Pray, Mister Rat, will you go with me?"
Heigh ho! says Rowley,
"Kind Mrs. Mousey for to see?"
With a rowley, powley, gammon and spinach,
Heigh ho! says Anthony Rowley.

They came to the door of Mousey's hall,
  Heigh ho! says Rowley,
They gave a loud knock, and they gave a loud call.
  With a rowley, powley, gammon and spinach,
  Heigh ho! says Anthony Rowley.

"Pray, Mrs. Mouse, are you within?"
  Heigh ho! says Rowley,
"Oh yes, kind sirs, I'm sitting to spin."
  With a rowley, powley, gammon and spinach,
  Heigh ho! says Anthony Rowley.

"Pray, Mrs. Mouse, will you give us some beer?"
  Heigh ho! says Rowley,
"For Froggy and I are fond of good cheer."
  With a rowley, powley, gammon and spinach,
  Heigh ho! says Anthony Rowley.

"Pray, Mr. Frog, will you give us a song?"
  Heigh ho! says Rowley,
"Let it be something that's not very long."
  With a rowley, powley, gammon and spinach,
  Heigh ho! says Anthony Rowley.

"Indeed, Mrs. Mouse," replied Mr. Frog,
  Heigh ho! says Rowley,
"A cold has made me as hoarse as a dog."
  With a rowley, powley, gammon and spinach,
  Heigh ho! says Anthony Rowley.

"Since you have a cold, Mr. Frog," Mousey said,
  Heigh ho! says Rowley,
"I'll sing you a song that I have just made."
  With a rowley, powley, gammon and spinach,
  Heigh ho! says Anthony Rowley.

But while they were all a-merry-making,
  Heigh ho! says Rowley,
A cat and her kittens came tumbling in.
  With a rowley, powley, gammon and spinach,
  Heigh ho, says Anthony Rowley.

The cat she seized the rat by the crown,
  Heigh ho! says Rowley,
The kittens they pulled the little mouse down.
  With a rowley, powley, gammon and spinach,
  Heigh ho! says Anthony Rowley.

This put Mr. Frog in a terrible fright,
Heigh ho! says Rowley,
He took up his hat and he wished them good night.
With a rowley, powley, gammon and spinach,
Heigh ho! says Anthony Rowley.

But as Froggy was crossing over a brook,
Heigh ho! says Rowley,
A lily-white duck came and gobbled him up.
With a rowley, powley, gammon and spinach,
Heigh ho! says Anthony Rowley.

So there was an end of one, two, three,
  Heigh ho! says Rowley,
The rat, the mouse, and the little frog-ee.
  With a rowley, powley, gammon and spinach,
  Heigh ho! says Anthony Rowley.

The Terrible Mr. Twitmeyer

by LILIAN MOORE *and* LEONE ADELSON

illustrated by PAUL GALDONE

THE STRANGE DOG CATCHER OF WEST BROOK

Wherever there are people there are towns.

Wherever there are towns there are dogs.

And where there are dogs there are dog catchers—like Mr. Twitmeyer.

Mr. Twitmeyer was the dog catcher for the town of West Brook. It was his job to catch all the dogs in West Brook that no one wanted any more.

He caught sick dogs and took them away.

He caught all the dogs that were left behind when people moved.

He caught dogs that would fight and dogs that would bite, and dogs that barked all night, keeping everyone awake.

Every once in a while someone called Mr. Twitmeyer on the telephone to tell him to come quickly and take a dog away.

Then Mr. Twitmeyer got into his little black truck, left his farm way out in the country, and drove fast to West Brook.

When he found the dog he locked it up in the back of his truck—

AND THAT DOG WAS NEVER SEEN AGAIN!

What happened to the dogs that Mr. Twitmeyer took away?

Nobody knew! He never told anyone what he did with them.

That was Mr. Twitmeyer's secret.

And of course the dogs could not tell either. Off they would go, barking and yelping, in the little black truck, never to be seen again.

People wondered. They would ask one another, "What *does* he do with those dogs?" But if they asked Mr. Twitmeyer he would only give them a strange look.

"You want to get rid of 'em, don't you? Well, I get rid of 'em for you." And that's all he would say.

What did that strange look mean?

What terrible things did Mr. Twitmeyer do to the dogs that nobody wanted any more?

People began to be a little afraid of him. When they saw

his black truck on the street, they called out to their own dogs.

"Here, Rover, come into the house this minute!"

"Here, Laddie—good dog. Quick, come get your bone!"

Then they locked up their dogs until that terrible Mr. Twitmeyer went away. They really did not need to worry, because Mr. Twitmeyer never took a dog away unless someone asked him to. And you may be very sure that no one asked him to unless there was just nothing else to do.

So Mr. Twitmeyer went on catching dogs and keeping his secret, and maybe to this day no one would have found out what it was if the Noddins hadn't bought a dog.

THE DEAR LITTLE PUPPY

One day Mr. and Mrs. Noddin went by the pet store, and in the window they saw a tiny brown puppy. It was a dear little puppy, so soft and round that Mr. and Mrs. Noddin both said at once, "What a nice dog for the children!" and they brought the dog home for Sara and Tom.

Everyone loved the little puppy. She was so soft and so roly-poly and such fun to hold!

"She's just a tiny butterball," said Sara, holding her close.

And that's what everyone called her after that—little Butterball.

But just when the Noddins got used to having a sweet, soft, round, roly-poly little dog around the house, Butterball

began to grow. She grew and grew.

First Butterball grew bigger than Tom.

"Golly!" said Tom.

Then she grew bigger than Sara.

"Oh, my!" said Sara.

And still she grew. Soon she grew bigger than her doghouse.

"Goodness!" said Mrs. Noddin.

Then she grew almost as big as Mr. Noddin and twice as strong.

Mr. Noddin said nothing. He just looked at Butterball and shook his head.

Sweet! Soft! Round and roly-poly! Where was the dear little puppy that had looked like a butterball? What they had now was a big, rough, noisy dog.

When she ran to say hello to anyone she almost knocked him over. When she jumped up to play with people she frightened them. When she was tied up, she barked so loud and so long that the Noddins were afraid all West Brook would hear her. And they did!

"Butterball indeed!" the neighbors said.

Now it is true that Butterball was big and rough and noisy, but inside she felt just as friendly and playful as when she had been a little puppy. She didn't mean to knock anyone over. She didn't mean to frighten anyone. She just liked people!

And she didn't mean to get into that trouble at the firehouse. It all started because she wanted so much to help.

Butterball loved the firehouse. It was always an exciting place to visit. When the firebell rang, Butterball hardly

knew what to do first. She wanted to do everything, to be everywhere, and to help everybody. She ran around and around, barking with excitement. She picked up firemen's boots and hats, and ran from one fireman to another trying to help them dress. Soon Fireman Jones had two right boots and Fireman Brown had two left boots. Fireman Miller had a big hat for his small head, and Fireman Santo had a small hat for his big head. When they all began yelling at Butterball she thought they were saying, "Thanks for helping us," so she would run around even faster, barking even louder.

And of course, when the fire truck went rolling into the street, there was Butterball right at the front wheels to show the way. The driver would shout at her, "Get out of the way!" and Butterball would keep barking back, "This way, men! This way!" For, after all, how could they get to a fire without her help?

When at last they did get to the fire, there was Butterball, right beside the Fire Chief, of course, helping as hard as she could. For some reason this always upset the Fire Chief very much. And one day, when Butterball got so mixed up in the hose that the water landed full on the Fire Chief instead of on the fire— WELL!

That was the day the Fire Chief called Mr. Noddin on the telephone and they had a long talk. That is, the Fire Chief did the talking. Mr. Noddin just listened. He moved the telephone as far away from his ear as he could, but he could still hear the Fire Chief's loud angry voice.

After that, Mr. Noddin took Butterball by the collar, pulled her out to the yard, and tied her up.

"And keep away from the firehouse from now on," the children heard him shout. "You great big—big—pest! If I hear of any more monkey business at the firehouse I'll give you to Mr. Twitmeyer."

Mr. Twitmeyer! The children could not believe their ears. Give Butterball to Mr. Twitmeyer! They threw themselves at their father.

"No, Daddy!" they screamed. "Don't let Mr. Twitmeyer take Butterball! Please! She'll be good! We'll watch her!"

BUTTERBALL GETS ANOTHER CHANCE

Butterball seemed to know that the children were worried, so she tried very hard to be good. She stayed near the house every day, and played with Sara and Tom. This made Mr. Noddin very happy.

He was so pleased with Butterball that one evening he thought he would take her for a walk. It was a nice quiet evening, just right for a nice quiet walk. People were sitting outside their houses, enjoying the pleasant air. As they walked past, Mr. Noddin and Butterball would say hello, or stop and visit for a minute. It was just the kind of quiet evening Mr. Noddin enjoyed most after a hard day at work.

But suddenly there was a loud CLANG-CLANG-CLANG! Butterball stood still. Her ears went up at the lovely sound of the fire bell. CLANG-CLANG! Then another sound—DONG-DONG, DONG-DONG! That would be the fire truck. Why, they couldn't have a fire without her! Goodness! She would have to hurry!

So off went Butterball! And off went Mr. Noddin, too! Not that Mr. Noddin liked fires, but he was holding tight to Butterball's strap, and he couldn't help himself. With one hand he held on to his hat, and with the other he held

on to Butterball.

People running to watch the fire engine go by, saw Mr. Noddin go flying down the street. They thought the poor man had gone crazy. As he went rushing by, his old friend, Mr. Green, saw him.

"Hey, there, Noddin!" he called out. "Aren't you a little too old to go chasing fire trucks? Ha-ha-ha!"

But poor Mr. Noddin couldn't stop to answer. He had all he could do to hold on to Butterball. And when they got to the fire, he had all he could do to get her away.

It was late that evening when Mr. Noddin and Butterball got home from what had started as a quiet little walk.

"Did you have a nice time, dear?" asked Mrs. Noddin.

At first all Mr. Noddin could say was something that sounded like, "Dang-ding-dang-dang-BLAST!"

When at last he could talk, he told his family just what he thought of Butterball. He ended up by saying, "And this time we've just got to do something about that dog, or we send for Mr. . . ."

"No!" the children screamed. "Not Mr. Twitmeyer, Daddy!" And they began to cry.

"All right, all right!" said Mr. Noddin. "I'm ashamed to walk down Main Street again, or look Bob Green in the face, but I suppose we have to give that fool dog another chance. Only, what's to be done with her? We have to find some way to keep her home."

They all sat and thought. "I know," said Sara. "We can teach her to go fetch things. Then she will be more like a house dog, and she can help us lots."

"All right," said Mr. Noddin. "It's about time she was of some use around here. We'll teach her to bring my slippers to me when I come home, and carry the newspaper in, and things like that."

Everyone was happy about the new idea—Butterball most of all. The family was surprised to see how fast she

learned to fetch and carry. Soon she was bringing Mr. Noddin his slippers every evening and carrying in the newspaper every morning. It was fun for Butterball, for each time she brought something she got a pat on the head. She could see how pleased they all were with her new tricks.

Best of all, Mr. Noddin was no longer cross with her. Well, if that was all it took to keep her family happy—just to fetch them things—why, that was easy. She would have to show them what she could do when she really put her mind to it.

BUTTERBALL LEARNS TO FETCH

One rainy night, Mr. Noddin came home so wet that he had to change all his clothes before supper.

"It certainly is a terrible night," he said as he sat down to eat. "The rain is coming down in buckets. I thought I'd have to swim the last two blocks. It's good to be home on a night like this. Where's Butterball with my slippers?"

"I let her out a little while ago," said Mrs. Noddin. "She'll be back soon for her supper, I guess."

Supper was almost over when the Noddins heard a noise at the front door.

"That must be Butterball," said Sara. "I'll let her in."

Butterball ran through the door right to Mr. Noddin's chair. They could see she was excited about something. Her eyes were shining, her tail was wagging fast, and she was giving sharp, happy little barks. She took Mr. Noddin's coat in her teeth and pulled.

"Oh, what a surprise I have for you," she seemed to say. "Hurry up!"

Running from one to the other, she got the family to follow her to the porch door. Mrs. Noddin turned on the light so they could all see better, and Butterball gave a sharp little bark, as if to say, "There! Just look at that!"

Mrs. Noddin did—and then she let out a scream. There, in the middle of the porch was a big pile of wet things—big and little things, new and old things, important and not-so-important things, and. . . .

NOT ONE OF THEM BELONGED TO THE NODDINS!

"That's Bobby Heller's baseball glove!" cried Tom.

"And here's Ellen's new doll!" Sara said.

"And Mrs. Hill's umbrella! And I-don't-know-whose shoes and rubbers!" cried Mrs. Noddin. "Oh, dear! Whatever shall we do?"

Well, there really was nothing to do but to start returning the things Butterball had brought home. Mr. Noddin spent the whole evening tramping back and forth in the wind and rain with the neighbors' things. He was very tired.

Mrs. Noddin spent the whole evening on the telephone

telling the neighbors how sorry she was. She was very tired too.

And Butterball! She was not only tired—she was sad.

After all, it had been a lot of work carrying all those things from houses up and down the street. And not even to get one tiny pat on the head! Now really! It was too bad.

What Mr. and Mrs. Noddin thought—well! The less said about that the better.

If the children had not cried so hard Mr. Noddin would have called Mr. Twitmeyer then and there. Once again Butterball was given another chance.

BUTTERBALL LEARNS TO JUMP

It was very clear that Butterball could not be left free to visit the firehouse or to take the neighbors' things again. But if they tied her up they must give her something to do. Something that a big, strong, playful dog would like to do. What could it be?

Mr. Noddin thought for a long time. Then he went to work.

First he put up a high fence to keep Butterball in the back yard. Then he tied a rope between two poles. On this rope he hung strong rags—some short and some long. Mr. Noddin hoped that when Butterball saw them swinging in the wind she would jump for them.

And that was just what she did. She loved the new game. Not only did she jump for the rags, but she hung on to them with her strong white teeth, swinging back and forth. She liked to see how high she could jump. She liked to see how long she could hang on before she let go. In this way, she had something to keep her busy and happy inside her fence.

Yes, it was a very good idea, but Butterball became a better jumper than Mr. Noddin had planned. For one day she gave a jump that took her over the fence—right into Mrs. Miller's back yard! Perhaps on any other day Butterball might have jumped right back over the fence to go on playing.

But this was washday, and Mrs. Miller had a nice big line full of clean wash hanging in her yard. There were big sheets and towels, shirts and overalls, and all kinds of underwear—pink and white, long and short. How nicely they flapped in the wind!

Ah-h-h-h! thought Butterball.

She tried the sheets first, but Rip!—they weren't very strong. Then the towels. Rip-Zip! Why, they weren't very strong, either. Oh, dear! The shirts weren't any better! Now, the long underwear—that was more fun. She got one or two good swings before that, too, went Zip-Rip-Zip!

Mrs. Noddin didn't know that Butterball was visiting her neighbor until she heard Mrs. Miller screaming, "Help! Stop! Stop!"

Mrs. Noddin ran out as fast as she could, just in time to see Butterball make her last jump. It had to be the last jump, for as Butterball came down, so did the whole wash line and all the nice, clean wash.

A SAD DAY FOR THE NODDINS

The next day Mr. Twitmeyer came for Butterball. It was a sad day indeed for the Noddins, but by now there was nothing else that could be done.

"Mr. Twitmeyer will have to take either us or Butterball," said Mr. Noddin. "The neighbors will see to that."

So Mr. Twitmeyer came for Butterball, dressed as always in heavy boots and thick gloves, carrying his long rope. He was all ready for the big wild dog that he had been told about. But Butterball, friendly as ever and interested in everything, licked his face and jumped right up into the black truck to look around.

"Oh, Butterball, Butterball," Sara cried as she gave the dog a last hug. Tom put his head against Butterball's coat and whispered, "Good-bye, Butterball, I don't care what you've done. I love you anyway."

Even Mrs. Noddin felt tearful as Mr. Twitmeyer shut the door of his truck in Butterball's face and got ready to drive away.

"Please, Mr. Twitmeyer," she said, "won't you tell us

what you are going to do with our dog? We would feel so much better if we knew."

The dog catcher looked down at her and shook his head. "Maybe you would and maybe you wouldn't, ma'am," he said gruffly. And that's all he would say before he drove off.

The unhappy Noddins could only look after the truck and think: Poor, poor Butterball! To have to go with the terrible Mr. Twitmeyer! To go—no one knew where, or to what end. To know only that this strange black truck was taking her where she would never see her family again!

MR. TWITMEYER'S SECRET

Meanwhile, what *was* happening to Butterball?

She bumped around in the back of the truck for what seemed a very long time. She was beginning to feel tired, when the truck stopped and the back door opened. Mr. Twitmeyer looked in. It was the same Mr. Twitmeyer, and yet it wasn't. Gone were the gloves and the boots and the rope. Gone was the hat over his eyes, and the gruff look on his face. And Mr. Twitmeyer smiled at Butterball! He even patted her gently!

"Feel a little stiff, don't you?" he asked. "Well, we're safe now—we're far away from West Brook. You can come and sit up front with me."

Butterball jumped into the seat beside Mr. Twitmeyer, and on they went. As they rode, Mr. Twitmeyer talked to Butterball, patting her from time to time. Listening to his kind, friendly voice, Butterball felt happy.

Even if she didn't understand all the words, she knew she was with someone who would not hurt her. Now, that was no surprise to Butterball, but it would have been a great surprise to the people of West Brook. For that was Mr. Twitmeyer's secret. . . .

HE LOVED DOGS AS MUCH AS PEOPLE THOUGHT HE HATED THEM!

He told Butterball all about it. "It's this way," he said. "Lots of people think that it takes a mean man to catch mean, bad dogs. Well, it's not so, but I wouldn't tell 'em that. I just make believe I'm mean so I can keep my dog-catching job. If I keep my job I can be with dogs, and that's what I'd rather do than anything else. As soon as I get a dog away from West Brook we get to be real pals. Just like you and me, Butterball."

Butterball licked his ear, and said, "Woof!"

Mr. Twitmeyer laughed. "I just hope people don't find out that all I do with their dogs is keep them on my farm. I guess they wouldn't understand that. Wait 'til you get to the farm–you'll find a lot of your old friends there, all having the time of their lives."

The moment Butterball saw Mr. Twitmeyer's farm she loved it. It *was* a fine place for dogs. There was plenty of room to run and play, there were good things to eat, and a good place to sleep.

Best of all, Butterball found that, just as Mr. Twitmeyer had promised, many of her old friends were there, friends she had not seen for a long time.

They were the same, yet not quite the same. What was it that Mr. Twitmeyer did to these dogs that came to his farm? When a new dog came, Mr. Twitmeyer took him out every morning for a long walk and a long talk. He told him things, and he taught him things. That didn't seem like much, but after a while the dogs changed.

Take Sandy—Butterball used to play wth Sandy back in West Brook, but she had never liked him. Sandy had been mean. Butterball had never known when he would take her bone away.

And the same with Brownie, who used to live down the street. He had never learned to obey, but now he followed Mr. Twitmeyer around and did whatever he was told. Whatever it was that Mr. Twitmeyer did, it made the dogs feel so good inside that after a while they didn't want to be bad any more.

BUTTERBALL GETS HOMESICK

For about a week, Butterball was so busy getting to know the farm, playing with her friends, and taking her walks with Mr. Twitmeyer, that she had no time to think about anything else.

Then, one day, right in the middle of a game with four of her friends, Butterball had a funny feeling. She had to stop playing and sit down. It couldn't be that she was sick, because she had never felt better in her life.

Lady sat down beside her and gave a few sharp barks, as if to say, "What's the matter, Butterball? Have you got a sticker in your ear?"

The other dogs came over too, barking, jumping, and

trying to get Butterball to play. She tried—she tried hard, but she wasn't having any fun. She didn't feel sick, but she didn't feel quite right, either. What could the matter be?

She walked over to Mr. Twitmeyer and rubbed against him. Then she gave a sad little yelp, as if she were asking, "What's the matter with me, Mr. Twitmeyer?"

He patted her head gently. "Poor Butterball," he said. "You'll get over it. They all do. The trouble with you is that you want to see Sara and Tom and the Noddins again. But I'm afraid that's the one thing you can't do."

The only words that Butterball understood were "Sara and Tom," but as soon as she heard them, she knew what her trouble was. She must see her family again! Not that she wanted to leave Mr. Twitmeyer forever. Oh, no! She just wanted to visit the Noddins to see that all was well with them.

Butterball loved Mr. Twitmeyer, and she wouldn't have made trouble for him for anything in the world. The one thing she did not understand was that to keep his job, Mr. Twitmeyer had to keep his secret. And to keep his secret, no dog that he took away from West Brook could ever be seen there again!

Because she did not understand this, Butterball made up her mind to go home for a little visit—just a day or so. As soon as she told that to herself she felt happy again and ran barking the news to her friends.

At first, none of them would believe her. Then a funny thing began to happen. One by one, Sandy and Lady and Brownie and Pooch sat down around Butterball, looking a little sad.

Sandy made an unhappy little noise. Was he thinking of home, too?—of Baby Sue, perhaps, who used to love to pull his tail?

Brownie gave a lonely howl. Maybe he was thinking of Jimmie and the fun they used to have chasing baseballs.

The five dogs gave five deep sighs.

All at once Pooch looked at Lady.

Lady looked at Sandy.

Sandy looked at Brownie.

Then they each gave an excited bark, which said, "Let's. . . . !"

And while Mr. Twitmeyer was busy in the barn, off they went, the five of them, down the long dusty road back to West Brook.

If you had happened to be walking down Main Street late that afternoon, you would have seen a strange sight. Down the street came five dogs—long and short, big and little—one behind the other. You could see they were very tired, for their ears and tails hung down and they were breathing hard. Every once in a while the smallest dog sat down as if to say, "I just can't take another step!" Then the other dogs sat down, too, to wait for her.

On they went until they got to Green-Tree Street. Turning the corner here, they stopped, looking about them with tired eyes. Then, suddenly, barking and yelping, they dashed across the street. People, frightened, ran to get out of their way. Someone even yelled, "Watch out! Wild dogs!"

But of course they were not wild—just very thirsty. All they wanted was a drink. It had been a long hot trip from Mr. Twitmeyer's farm, without any water on the way. And there, right across the street, was a pretty fountain with lots of nice cool water spilling into a pool and sparkling in the sun.

How were they to know that this fountain had just been put up by the Mayor of West Brook? How were they to know how proud he was of his beautiful new fountain? And how could they know that it stood right outside the window of his office?

Splash! Splash! Splash! How cool! How good!

When the dogs had all they could drink, they jumped in to cool off. When they had cooled off, they stayed in to have fun. In and out they jumped, splashing and running after each other in the water.

People stopped to look, and soon there was quite a crowd around the fountain, many of them yelling at the dogs to make them go away. Suddenly a window opened and the Mayor called out, "What's going on down there? Can't you see I'm trying to work?"

Then he saw the dogs!

Not one dog! Not two dogs—but what seemed to the angry Mayor like dozens of dogs playing in his beautiful new fountain. Bang! Down came the window, and in a minute out came the Mayor himself.

"Get those dogs out of there!" he shouted. Everyone got busy trying to catch the dogs, but the dogs seemed to think it was a lot of fun. After a while it was hard to tell who was wetter—the dogs or the people.

"Get Mr. Twitmeyer!" the Mayor cried, trying to dry himself with his handkerchief. "Somebody go and telephone Twitmeyer! Whose dogs are they, anyway?"

"I think I know that little dog!" a woman called out. "But Twitmeyer took her away long ago—she was a chicken chaser."

"Nonsense!" yelled the Mayor. "If Twitmeyer took her away, she couldn't be here, could she?"

"But, Mr. Mayor," said a little girl, pulling on the Mayor's coat, "that big dog is Butterball Noddin, and Mr. Twitmeyer took her away, too."

Someone thought the white dog had belonged to the Fuller family. Someone else said he was sure that the brown dog was the one who used to chase cars on his street before the dog catcher took him away. Everybody began talking and shouting at once.

To make matters worse, the fire truck went screaming by and no one could hear what anyone else was saying. At last the Mayor, by shouting the loudest of all, got everyone to listen to him.

"I'm sure you're all making a big mistake," he said. "West Brook has a fine dog catcher. When Mr. Twitmeyer takes a dog away—well, that's the end of *him!*"

The little girl pulled on the Mayor's coat. "That *is* Butterball Noddin, Mr. Mayor," she said again.

The Mayor got very angry. "Go away, little girl!" he shouted. "Now, then, get those dogs out of there! Where's Twitmeyer? Didn't someone go for Twitmeyer?" He shook his finger at the dogs. "Wait 'til the dog catcher comes!" he cried. "Just you wait!"

THE SECRET IS OUT

At that moment all the dogs began to bark at once. They jumped out of the fountain, running to meet a black truck that had just pulled up. Slowly Mr. Twitmeyer got out of the truck.

To everyone's surprise, the dogs did not run away from the dog catcher. No, indeed! Instead, they jumped up and tried to lick his hands and face! They ran around him and rolled at his feet! It was hard to believe, but they were trying to show Mr. Twitmeyer how glad they were to see him.

"Down, Butterball," said Mr. Twitmeyer quietly. "Sit, Lady, Brownie, Pooch, Sandy. Good dogs." And the five excited dogs sat right down again, looking happily at Mr. Twitmeyer.

But if ever a man looked unhappy, it was Mr. Twitmeyer.

He looked as if West Brook were the last place in the world he wanted to be. He said a few words to the dogs and they sat down quietly beside the truck while he walked up to the Mayor.

"For goodness' sake!" the Mayor cried. "Twitmeyer—those dogs—they seem to know you! Do you know them?"

The dog catcher looked down at his feet. "Yes, Mr. Mayor," he said in a low voice. "I—I guess so. They—er—they belong to me."

The little girl cried out, "Oooh, they do not! That big one is Butterball Noddin—I know!"

The Mayor stamped his foot. "Will someone *please* take that little girl away!"

"But it's true, sir," said the unhappy Mr. Twitmeyer.

"What's true?" shouted the Mayor. "What do you mean —'it's true'? How did these dogs get here? And what are they doing here—playing in my fountain—I mean, our fountain? Twitmeyer, what *does* all this mean?"

"Mr. Mayor," said Mr. Twitmeyer, "I never thought those dogs would ever be seen in West Brook again. I'm terribly sorry this happened, but from now on I'll be sure to keep the others locked up on my. . . ."

At that, the Mayor got very excited. He took off his hat and began to fan his face very fast.

"Others!" he cried. "What others are you talking about, Twitmeyer? Talk up, man, talk up!"

"Why," said Mr. Twitmeyer in a low voice, "why, I mean all the other dogs I've taken away from West Brook. I keep them down at my farm, you see."

The Mayor could hardly believe his ears. Whoever heard of a dog catcher who kept a farm full of dogs—dogs that nobody wanted? He came close to Mr. Twitmeyer and looked hard at him.

"Do you mean to tell me," he said, "that we pay you to do away with our bad dogs, and you *keep* them? What for, may I ask? Whatever *for?*"

"I like them," Mr. Twitmeyer told him. "And they're not bad dogs, you know."

"Oh, they're not, eh!" the Mayor cried. "I suppose *good*

dogs play in fountains and splash people! And I suppose *good* dogs chase chickens and fire engines! And I suppose. . . ."

In the midst of the Mayor's excitement a car pulled up and a little boy got out and looked around.

"Where is she?" he wanted to know. "Where's my dog?"

MR. TWITMEYER'S NEW SECRET

It was Tom Noddin and all the other Noddins. At the sound of Tom's voice Butterball jumped to her feet, wagging her tail as hard as she could. Then, with a WOOF! she rushed to the boy and covered him with kisses. Her happy barks filled the air. It was hard to tell who was more joyful—Butterball or the Noddins.

Soon the family heard the whole story of the runaway dogs.

"Oh, darling Butterball!" cried Sara. "We've missed you so much!"

"Butterball must have missed us too," added Mr. Noddin proudly. "Did you ever hear of a dog coming all this way to get back to her family? We'll never let you go again, Butterball."

"I don't understand this," said the Mayor, puzzled. "If you love that dog so much, why did you tell Twitmeyer to take her away?"

"Well," said Mrs. Noddin, "she got into trouble so much that we got angry one day. It all started because she used to chase the fire truck, and. . . ."

Mr. Twitmeyer went to the big dog and patted her head.

"Don't worry," he said with a smile. "She won't do that any more."

"How do you know that, Twitmeyer?" the Mayor asked. "How can I believe anything you say now?"

Mr. Twitmeyer looked very hurt. "Well," he began, "I. . . ."

"Why, he's right!" someone called out. "The fire truck came by here before and that dog didn't even move!"

The dog catcher looked up quickly. A few people nodded. "Yes," they said. "That's true!"

Mr. Twitmeyer was very pleased. So were the Noddins. But the Mayor looked as if he still didn't quite believe it.

"Twitmeyer," he said, "are you sure that Butterball won't chase the fire truck any more?"

"I know she won't," the dog catcher answered. "And

what's more, I don't think she will get into any other kind of trouble either."

"That's wonderful!" cried Mrs. Noddin. "We're so glad to have our dog back."

"They weren't all bad dogs," said Mr. Twitmeyer proudly. "Most of them just needed to be trained, that's all."

The woman who knew Lady gave a little sniff. "I suppose you trained Lady not to run after chickens, too, didn't you?" she called out.

"Yes, ma'am," Mr. Twitmeyer told her. "I did! After a couple of weeks on my farm she didn't even look at my chickens. You see," he said, turning to the Mayor, "I've always loved dogs. Seems I understand them, and they understand me."

The Mayor looked thoughful. "They *did* listen to you, and they did what you told them to. I saw that myself," he said. "But why didn't you ever tell me that you knew how to train dogs?"

For the first time Mr. Twitmeyer laughed. "You didn't ask me," he said. "You just told me to catch them." Everyone laughed along with Mr. Twitmeyer.

"You were good at keeping your secret," said the Mayor. "But now that we know, I'm afraid you can't be dog catcher for West Brook any more."

Mr. Twitmeyer looked very sad. "That's what I was afraid of," he said.

"No," the Mayor went on, "you can't be our dog catcher any more, Twitmeyer." Then he smiled. "But how would you like a new job? How would you like to be West

Brook's new dog trainer?"

Mr. Twitmeyer got red. Then he got white. Then he took off his old hat and looked at it and put it on again—backwards. Then he blew his nose in his old blue handkerchief. At last he spoke.

"Mr. Mayor," he said slowly, "and people of West Brook, I—I just don't know what to say."

"Hurray!" someone cried, and then everyone shouted, "Hurray for Twitmeyer! Hurray for the new dog trainer!"

But Mr. Twitmeyer did not seem to hear them. He was looking hard at his little black truck. He was thinking how fine WEST BROOK DOG TRAINER would look instead of WEST BROOK DOG CATCHER. Now he could call his farm WEST BROOK TRAINING SCHOOL FOR DOGS. Now he could do what he had wanted to do all his life.

AND HE WOULDN'T HAVE TO BE AFRAID THAT PEOPLE WOULD
FIND OUT!

Slowly he turned and smiled at all the people watching him. Then he looked at the five dogs and they began to wag their tails.

"Come here, Butterball," he said. Butterball came trotting over and Mr. Twitmeyer patted her head. "This is all your doing," he said. "If you hadn't become so homesick, I'd still be that terrible Mr. Twitmeyer. You gave away my secret, didn't you?"

"It's just as well," said the Mayor. "But now that old secret is out, I wish you'd tell me one thing."

"Surely, Mr. Mayor," said Mr. Twitmeyer happily. "Anything you want to know, just ask me."

"Well, it's this," said the Mayor. "How do you get those dogs to do just what you want them to?"

Everyone turned to watch Mr. Twitmeyer as they waited for his answer. How *did* he train those dogs? At last they would find out.

"Well, Mr. Mayor," Mr. Twitmeyer said slowly, "it's like this . . ." Then he began to laugh. "No," he said. "I won't tell you. Suppose we let that be my new secret!"

Toads and Diamonds

by CHARLES PERRAULT

illustrated by ALDREN WATSON

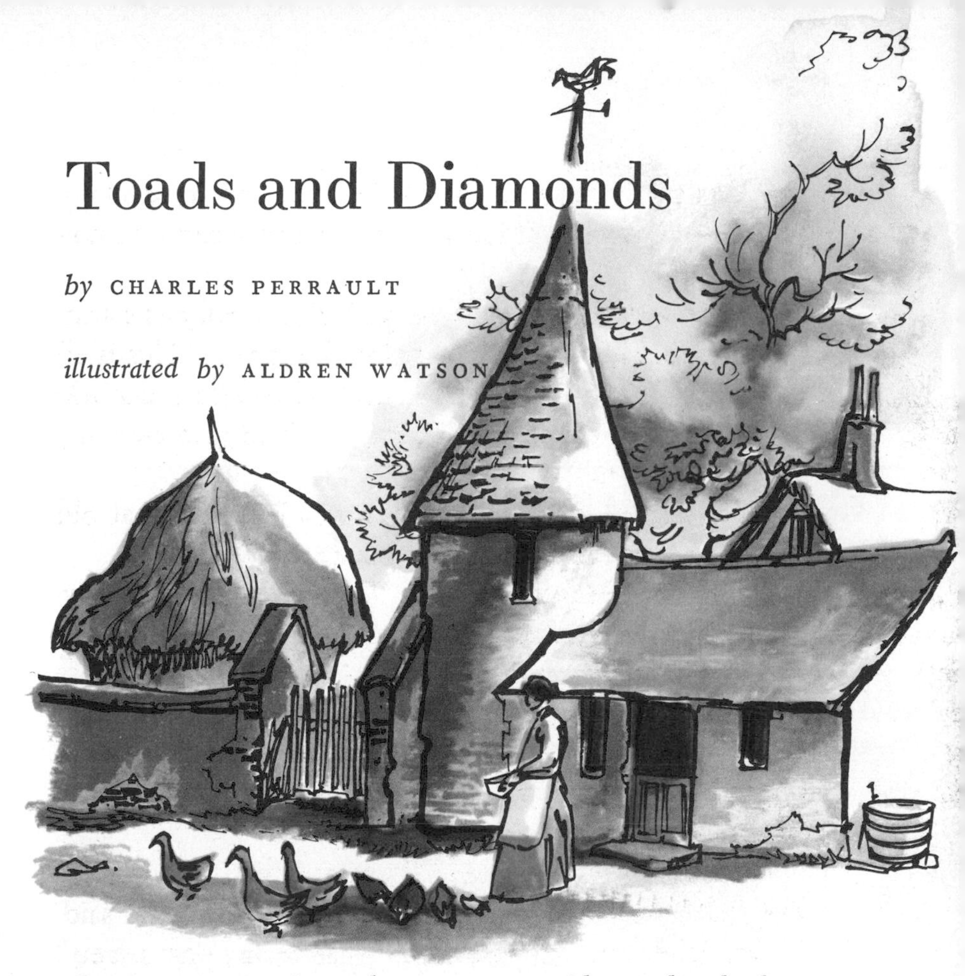

Once upon a time there was a widow who had two daughters. The elder was so much like her in face and disposition that whoever looked upon the daughter saw the mother. They were both so disagreeable and so proud there was no living with them.

The younger, who was the very picture of her father for courtesy and sweetness of temper, was withal one of the most beautiful girls ever seen. As people naturally love their own likeness, this mother doted on her elder daughter, and at the same time had a horrible aversion for the

younger. She made her eat in the kitchen and work continually.

Among the other things, this poor child was forced twice a day to draw water nearly a mile and a half from the house, and bring home a pitcher full of it. One day, as she was at the fountain, there came to her a poor woman, who begged her for a drink.

"Oh, ay, with all my heart, Goody," said this pretty girl. And immediately rinsing the pitcher, she took up some water from the clearest part of the fountain, and gave it to the woman, holding up the pitcher all the while that she might drink the easier.

The good woman, having drunk, said to her, "You are so very pretty, my dear, so good, and so mannerly, I cannot help giving you a gift." For this was a fairy who had taken the form of a poor countrywoman, to see how far the kindness and good manners of this pretty girl would go. "I will give you this gift:" continued the fairy, "at every word you speak, there shall drop from your mouth either a flower or a jewel."

When the pretty girl came home her mother scolded her for staying so long at the fountain.

"I beg your pardon, Mamma," said the poor girl, "for not making more haste." And in speaking these words, out of her mouth dropped two roses, two pearls, and two diamonds.

"What is it I see!" said her mother, astonished. "I think I see pearls and diamonds coming out of the girl's mouth! How happens this, child?"

This was the first time she had ever called her "child."

The poor girl told her frankly all that had happened, not without dropping infinite numbers of diamonds.

"In good faith," cried the mother, "I must send my elder child thither. Come, look what comes out of your sister's mouth when she speaks. Would you not be glad, my dear, to have the same gift given to you? You have nothing to do but draw water out of the fountain, and when a certain poor woman asks you to let her drink, to give it her very politely."

"It would be a strange sight indeed," said this ill-bred minx, "to see *me* draw water."

"You shall go, hussy," said the mother, "and this minute."

So she went, but grumbling all the way, taking with her the best silver tankard in the house. She was no sooner at the fountain than she saw coming out of the wood a lady most gloriously dressed, who came up to her and asked to drink. This was the very fairy who appeared to her sister, but had now taken the air and dress of a princess, to see how far this girl's rudeness would go.

"Am I come hither," said the proud, saucy girl, "to serve you with water, pray? I suppose the silver tankard was brought for your ladyship? However, you may drink out of it if you care to."

"You are not over and above polite," answered the fairy calmly. "And therefore, since you have such bad manners and are so unkind, I give you this gift: at every word you speak there shall drop from your mouth a frog or a toad."

So the proud girl returned home; and her mother, as soon as she saw her, cried, "Well, Daughter?"

"Well, Mother?" was the rude answer, and as the words were spoken, out of the girl's mouth dropped two toads and two frogs.

"Oh, mercy!" cried the mother. "What is it I see? Frogs and toads! Oh, that wretch, your sister, has caused all this. But she shall pay for it!" And immediately the mother began to beat her younger daughter.

The poor child fled away from her and went to hide herself in the depths of the forest. And there the King's son, on his return from hunting, found her. Seeing her so pretty, he asked what she did there alone and why she cried.

"Alas, sir, my mother has turned me out of doors."
The King's son, who saw five or six pearls and as many diamonds drop from her lips, desired her to tell him how that happened. She thereupon told him the whole story.

The King's son fell in love with her; and thinking to himself that such quantities of jewels were worth far more than the dowry of a rich princess, he conducted her to the palace of the King, his father, and there married her.

As for the proud elder sister, she soon found the frogs and toads such a nuisance that she never spoke again. So she and her mother lived very glumly together all the days of their lives.

Crunch Crunch

written and illustrated by

ETHEL *and* LEONARD KESSLER

Good Morning.

GOOD MORNING!

Everybody is ready for breakfast...

How about...

..YOU?

ME? . . .

I'm ready too!

We have eaten all the food. We need to buy some more . . .

So where do we go?

. . . to this great big STORE!

IN
OUT
BERRIES
2 lb 37¢
Sale
HANDLE WITH CARE

Let's take a cart (this one squeaks) . . . and fill it to the top . . .

Everybody ready? Let's shop!

Now—what do we need?

SHOPPING LIST
peanut butter
Jelly
Spaghetti
cheese
butter
ONE POUND
popcorn
eggs
peas
milk
sugar
SUGAR
oranges
tea
TEA
coffee for Daddy
COFFEE
cookies for ME

Cereal for breakfast—Soup for lunch

Chicken for supper—Potato chips to CRUNCH!

Now what else do we need?

1 pound of beans
5 pounds of potatoes
lettuce, bananas, apples,
onions and
2 pounds of tomatoes

Now I have a long, long wait while Mother buys the meat.

She puts the cold packages up against my feet!

Up and down and up and down until the shopping's done . . .

Up and down and around again . . .

I like this ride—it's FUN!

We stand in line. The register rings. The cashier takes the money.

But let's get home right away! Shopping makes me......

HUNGRY!

So, Crunch, Crunch—I think I'll have my lunch

Science Quizzes and Experiments

by JANE SHERMAN

illustrated by PETER SPIER

Text from *The Real Book of Amazing Scientific Facts,* copyright, 1953, by Franklin Watts, Inc., and published by Garden City Books.

The fact that a fact is a fact does not mean it is dull! Quizzes with scientific answers can be entertaining. Tricks to demonstrate scientific truths can be amusing. Here are some questions and some simple home experiments which you may use to amaze your friends while, at the same time, you have fun:

QUESTION: Is there any place in the Western Hemisphere where the sun rises in the Pacific Ocean?

ANSWER: Yes. In certain parts of the Isthmus of Panama, the sun rises in the Pacific and sets in the Atlantic. This is because the Isthmus curves in such a way that the end farthest to the east touches the Pacific Ocean, while the end farthest to the west touches the Atlantic.

QUESTION: Shellac is obtained from pine trees, sea water, a scale insect, or coal tar?

ANSWER: A scale insect.

QUESTION: If you were to stand directly on top of the site of the North Pole, facing south, what direction would be on your left? On your right?

ANSWER: South would be the only direction to your left and right and all around you.

QUESTION: Where in the United States is there a large body of water that has no fish in it?

ANSWER: The Great Salt Lake in Utah. Its water is six times saltier than the ocean—so salty that no fish can live in it.

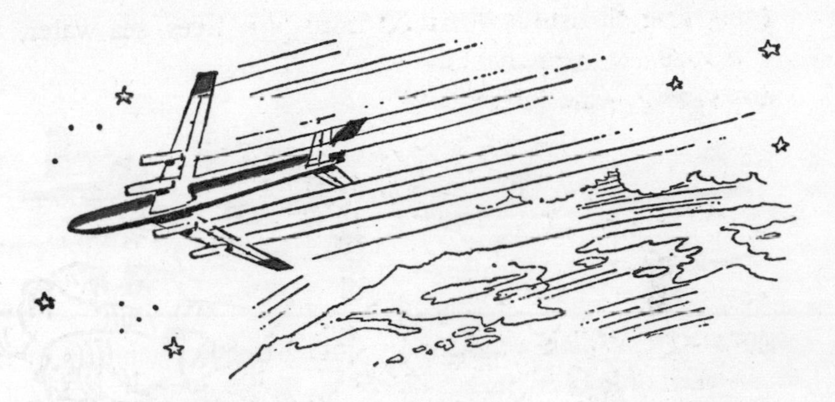

QUESTION: Suppose a plane could fly from New York to Los Angeles at a steady 1,000 miles per hour, without stopping. This distance is 3,500 miles, so the flight would take three and a half hours. If the plane left New York at noon, it would arrive in Los Angeles at 11:30 A.M. How is this possible?

ANSWER: The plane is moving toward the west faster than the earth is turning toward the east. This means the plane would continually fly faster than the sunlight as it reaches the earth. So the plane actually reaches the west a half an hour before the time it left the east, although it flew through the air for three and a half hours.

QUESTION: Which weighs more, a cubic foot of warm water, or a cubic foot of cold water?

ANSWER: The cold water weighs more because it has more molecules in it than warm water. One cubic foot of warm water weighs 61.998 pounds, while one cubic foot of cold water weighs 62.416 pounds. Water is heaviest at a temperature of 4 degrees Centigrade.

QUESTION: Which weighs more, a quart of heavy cream or a quart of light cream?

ANSWER: A quart of light cream weighs more than a quart of heavy cream because heavy cream contains more fat. This fat weighs less than its equivalent amount of liquid in the light cream. For this reason, cream rises to the top of a bottle of milk.

QUESTION: Cement and concrete are the same materials with two different names. True or false?

ANSWER: False. Cement is one of the ingredients of concrete. Concrete is made of a mixture of sand or gravel with water. It is hardened by cement which is used to bind the materials together.

QUESTION: If a rubber ball, a steel ball and a wooden ball of the same size are thrown with equal force on a sidewalk, which do you think will bounce the highest into the air?

ANSWER: The steel ball will bounce the highest, then the rubber one and lastly, the wooden one. This is because steel can be more quickly compressed and will more quickly return to its original shape than rubber. This compression (when the ball hits the sidewalk) and return to shape (which forces the ball up into the air) is what determines how high a ball will bounce. Rubber compresses easily, but it is comparatively slow in returning to its original size.

QUESTION: A mud puppy is a kind of mud-loving little dog. True or False?

ANSWER: False. A mud puppy is a large aquatic salamander.

QUESTION: What animal looks like a piece of rock?

ANSWER: Coral.

QUESTION: What animal can be used in your bath?

ANSWER: A sponge.

QUESTION: A sea elephant is an elephant that can swim. True or False?

ANSWER: False. A sea elephant is a kind of seal.

QUESTION: A laughing jackass is a kind of bird. True or false?

ANSWER: True.

QUESTION: A flying fox is a large tropical bat. True or False?

ANSWER: True.

QUESTION: Which animals get up with their hind legs first when they have been lying down?

ANSWER: Cattle, sheep, goats, antelope, deer, giraffes, and all members of the cud-chewing family rise with their hind legs first. All other large four-footed animals use their front legs first.

Your senses of touch and taste may usually be relied upon to tell you the truth. But not always. Try this on yourself, then on your friends. Close your eyes tight and hold your nose. Then ask someone to give you a bite of raw apple or a bite of raw potato without telling you which is which. You won't be able to tell whether you're tasting an apple or a potato.

QUESTION: Can an expert tell, by looking at a drop of blood through a microscope, whether that blood came from a Negro, a white man, an Indian, or a Chinese?

ANSWER: No. All human beings belong to the zoological species called *Homo sapiens*, and their blood is the same.

Here is another taste fooler: Take a clean, unpainted stick of wood. Open your mouth and very carefully touch the end of the wood to the back part of your tongue. The wood will taste bitter.

Now take the very same stick and touch its end to the tip of your tongue. The wood will taste sweet. At the sides of your tongue it will taste sour.

The wood really has no taste at all. But it tastes bitter or sweet or sour according to the taste buds located along your tongue.

Nor can you always believe what you feel with your fingers. To prove this fact, try the following: Take a marble and hold it between your crossed first and second fingers, as you see in the picture. Now close your eyes and roll the marble about on a table top, holding it always between your two crossed fingers so that it touches first one finger, then the other. Since you know there is only one marble, you would naturally expect to feel only one. But your sense of touch distinctly feels two marbles.

This odd fact was known to scientists more than two thousand years ago, but the reason for it is still not certain. It is believed that the unfamiliar sensation is interpreted incorrectly by the brain.

Here's an interesting demonstration of how air pressure works. Take a flat hard-rubber sink stopper, the kind that has a ring in its center. Wet the bottom of the stopper and place it on the seat of a flat-topped stool. Make sure there is no air between the seat and the stopper. Now tie a string through the stopper's ring. With the help of no other force except the pressure of the outside air upon the top of the sink stopper, you can then lift up the stool by the string.

Did you know that although iron window screening is about seven times as heavy as water, it can be made to float? To prove this, fill a bowl with water. Take a small square of screen and carefully lay it flat on the surface of the water. It will not only float there, but it will support the weight of a cork if you place the cork gently in the middle of the piece of screen.

But in order to make this "raft" sink all you have to do is dip a corner of a bar of soap in the bowl of water, without touching the screen.

The reason the iron floats in the first place is because the surface of the water "stretches" like a very, very thin elastic. Light, flat, waterproof articles can float on this elastic surface without breaking through it.

But certain substances, such as soap, lower this "surface tension," as it is called. So when you touch a bit of soap to the water, the screen sinks.

Speaking of soap, would you like to make a little model boat which will move across water without any sails or engine?

Cut a piece of cardboard in the shape of a boat with a pointed front and a square back. Make a small V-shaped cut in the square back, and place a tiny bit of soap in this V.

Now fill a bowl with water, and place your soap-powered boat on the water's surface. The boat will immediately begin to move all over the water in the basin until the surface tension is entirely weakened by the soap.

The secret behind this mystery motor lies in the bit of soap. As it dissolves, the soap weakens the surface tension of the water directly behind the boat. The tension directly ahead of it is stronger, so the boat is pulled forward onto the firmer "skin" of water. This continues until the soap has weakened the surface of all the water in the basin.

While you're in the kitchen, suppose you take a raw egg and a hard-boiled egg from the refrigerator. Do you know how to tell which is which?

Place each egg on a saucer. Now briskly spin the eggs, watching what each one does. The egg that is hard-boiled will spin steadily for quite a while. The raw egg will spin slowly, wobble around, then soon stop.

The reason for this behavior on the part of the raw egg is that it is filled with a semi-liquid, while the hard-boiled egg is solid. For complex physical reasons a solid substance tends to retain motion longer than a liquid substance does.

There is nothing useful about a glass full of dancing mothballs, unless your father happens to own a store and would like to place such an attraction in its window. But here is a simple experiment which is fun to do and to watch:

Fill a tall glass or transparent vase with water. Add one tablespoonful of white vinegar and stir. Then slowly add one half-teaspoonful of bicarbonate of soda. The mixture will immediately fizz. While it is still bubbling, drop five or six mothballs into the glass. Within a few minutes, one ball will slowly rise to the top of the water, stay there a second, then drop to the bottom. And they will repeat this fascinating "perpetual motion" every few minutes for several hours.

What is the "motor" that makes the mothballs move? Look at them closely. You will see that bubbles of carbon dioxide, made by the reaction of the vinegar to the baking soda, cling to the outside of the mothballs. Whenever these bubbles become large enough, they float the mothball to the surface of the water. There, some of the gas bubbles get knocked off, and down the mothball sinks—only to accumulate more gas bubbles and rise and sink again and again.

The next time you have some guests for dinner ask them this riddle-trick:

Here is an ice cube floating in a cup of water. And here is a short length of string. Using only the items usually found on a dinner table, without tying the string around the ice or using a spoon, can your remove the ice cube from the water?

If your guests say no, here's the way you can show them how to do the trick: Wet the end of the string and lay it across the ice cube. Then sprinkle a little salt along each side of the string. Within a few moments, the string becomes frozen fast to the ice cube, and you can easily lift it out of the cup.

Why? Because salt lowers the freezing point of the ice which it touches, causing it to melt. But when it melts, the salted ice steals heat from the rest of the ice and from the water on the string. And as heat is stolen from them, they freeze together.

And let's end these experiments with a real scientific mystery—an amazing trick for which there is as yet no completely accurate answer:

Fill a drinking glass to the brim with water, but not so full that the top rounds up above the edge of the glass. Keep a thin wire or a stiff broom straw at hand. Now take an ordinary table-size salt shaker that is full of salt. Stirring the water all the time with the thin wire or broom straw, slowly begin to pour the salt into the water. You can pour the entire contents of the salt shaker into the water in this way—without making the water overflow the rim of the glass!

Science really doesn't know yet how this is possible or why. It is believed that there may be spaces between the molecules that make up the water. And the molecules that make up the salt apparently can fit into these spaces without adding to the total volume. Perhaps this is a mystery you may help solve someday!

Let's Go to the South Sea Islands

Far out in the southwestern part of the great Pacific Ocean lies an island world called Oceania. It is better known as the South Sea Islands. There are thousands of islands in this area. Even today no one is sure just how many!

The islands are all sizes. Some are quite large; others are mere dots of land with only a few coconut palm trees. Most of the people live on the high islands where the soil is fertile. The low islands, especially the tiny atolls (long, circular coral reefs), are beautiful places, but dangerous when the Pacific typhoons blow.

The Polynesians, a brown-skinned, friendly people, live on lovely islands like Samoa, Tahiti, Tonga. A peaceful folk, they are famous seamen and navigators. The small islands of the Carolines, Marshalls, Marianas, and Gilberts are inhabited by a shorter, darker people called Micronesians. Negroes, or Melanesians, dwell closer to Australia on the Solomons, New Hebrides, New Caledonias, and Fiji Islands. There are some savage cannibals in the interior of these islands who have never seen a white man!

The South Sea Islands are rapidly changing, particularly since World War II. But most islanders live as they did years ago. They build thatched huts; grow yams, taros, bananas; get many products from the coconut; and take much of their living from the sea. And Oceania still possesses its eternal charm and tropical beauty.

Not long ago these friendly warriors on New Guinea were wild tribesmen. They are decorated for a tribal ceremony.

When people dream of paradise on a carefree island, they picture a lovely, peaceful shore like this one.

MARIANAS
GUAM
2
WAKE I.
12
7
BIKINI I.
MARSHALL ISLANDS
CAROLINE ISLANDS
PACIFIC
N
W
E
S
GILBERT ISLANDS
10
ADMIRALTY ISLANDS
8
NEW BRITAIN
SOLOMON ISLANDS
ELLICE ISLANDS
PHOE
TOKELA
NEW GUINEA
SANTA CRUZ ISLANDS
NEW HEBRIDES
3
FIJI ISLANDS
VANUA LEVU
VITI LEVU
SAMO ISLAN
TONGA ISLANDS
9
LOYALTY ISLANDS
NEW CALEDONIA
AUSTRALIA
NORFOLK I.
6
KERMADEC ISLANDS
NEW ZEALAND

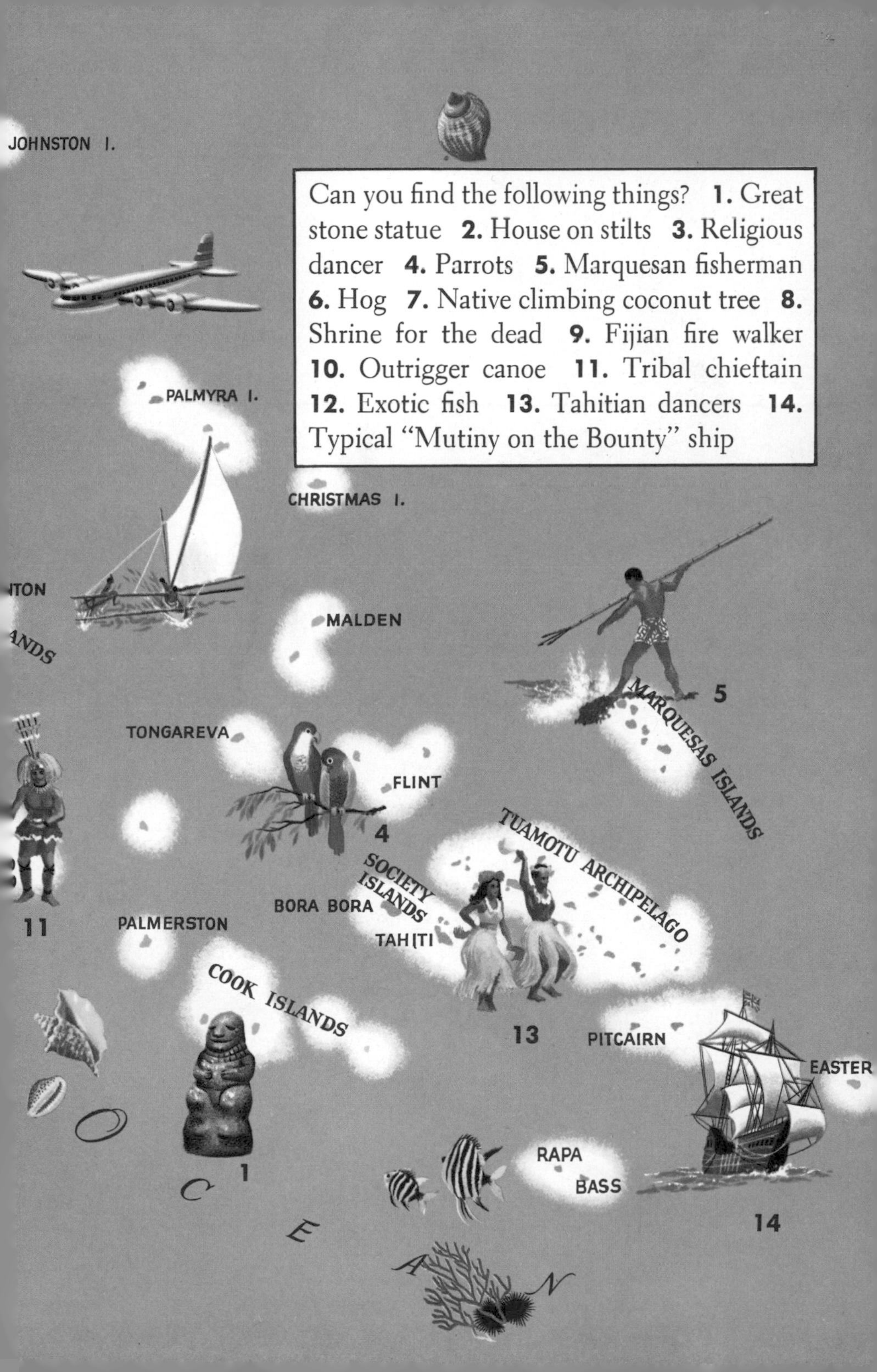
JOHNSTON I.
Can you find the following things? 1. Great stone statue 2. House on stilts 3. Religious dancer 4. Parrots 5. Marquesan fisherman 6. Hog 7. Native climbing coconut tree 8. Shrine for the dead 9. Fijian fire walker 10. Outrigger canoe 11. Tribal chieftain 12. Exotic fish 13. Tahitian dancers 14. Typical "Mutiny on the Bounty" ship
PALMYRA I.
CHRISTMAS I.
MALDEN
5
MARQUESAS ISLANDS
TONGAREVA
FLINT
4
TUAMOTU ARCHIPELAGO
SOCIETY ISLANDS
BORA BORA
TAHITI
11
PALMERSTON
COOK ISLANDS
13
PITCAIRN
EASTER
1
RAPA
BASS
14
O C E A N

These Micronesian houses are set in a grove of coconut trees. The coconut tree supplies fibre for the thatched roofs and sleeping mats, as well as food. The room inside the house is dark and damp, but people live mainly outdoors.

This old man is the chief of a village. He comes from a noble family.

A woman with a wood-carved *Tiki* which guards the entrance to a temple.